I0525646

Home for the Holidays

Cauldron Falls, Volume 3

Solara Gordon

Published by THE EARTH MOVED, LLC, 2023.

HOME FOR THE HOLIDAYS

First edition. December 17, 2023.

Copyright © 2023 Solara Gordon.

ISBN: 979-8988654933

Written by Solara Gordon.

Also by Solara Gordon

Watch for more at https://solaragordon.com/.

Thank you to the following members of my readers group and street team (Solara's Glamorous Stars) for inspiring characters, cheering them on, and letting me name characters after them: Amelia Pluck, Anna Mua Palakiko, Maggie Keiko, Chevy Allen, and Tara Black Finnerty. A special thank you to Christine Heydt for providing beta reading. Inspiration comes from many places. One of my main inspirations is my fabulous readers group and street team, Solara's Glamorous Stars. You're all awesome shining stars and wonderful inspirations. Here's to HOME FOR THE HOLIDAYS! May you laugh out loud, fall in love with more of Cauldron Falls citizens and cheer them on as they are HOME FOR THE HOLIDAYS!

Smiles,

Solara Gordon

ONE

Elana Jones stepped onto the jetway leading from the plane to the Cauldron Falls airport main terminal. Making her midmorning flight had gone smoothly until he boarded the plane. She'd put up with her colleagues fussing about a witch taking an early morning flight the day of the Solstice Sadie Hawkins full moon. Twenty-six years and more Sadie Hawkins full moons than she could easily count had come and gone. The matchmakers she'd taught, apprenticed, and recommended hadn't given second thoughts about why their instructor was still single. Elana glanced over her shoulder as she entered the main terminal. He was several passengers behind her. He'd passed her twice during the two-hour flight from Wichita River. Even with his glasses on, James Warren hadn't apparently recognized her.

James had furrowed his brow as he made his way down the aisle trying to read the seat and row tabs until he put his glasses on. Elana hoped he hadn't noticed her giving him a once-over hot glance. His ginger hair and beard were grayer than the last picture she'd seen of him five years ago. Was he still as vain about his looks? Fifteen years ago, he'd joked about coloring the gray patches peppering his beard and hair. Even then, he'd gotten her hot and bothered. Not that he noticed. James probably hadn't recognized her anyway. Her hair was shorter and completely gray. Cataract surgery eliminated her need for the glasses she'd worn the last time James had seen her.

Elana merged into the flow of passengers making their way to baggage claim. Hopefully, her niece Siobhan had found a parking space and wasn't circling the terminal. Two gates down, Elana stepped out of the flow of passengers. Her cell phone had buzzed twice. She took her tote off her shoulder, reaching inside as her cell phone buzzed again. Caller id showed Siobhan's number. Elana moved closer to the windows, pacing back and forth trying to

1

improve her reception. On her last turn, Siobhan answered as James walked by with his cell phone to his ear.

"Yes, Lance, I can rent a car. I know you're sorry you can't pick me up. You can stop apologizing. It's not like I'm writing you out of my will." James grinned as Lance stopped speaking. "I know how to get to your mom's place. My phone's got GPS and I'll get a car with navigation. See you there when you get home from work."

James ended the call before Lance could reply. His nephew had his moments. Lance's position on Cauldron Falls' police force took the family by surprise. Lance had never shown any desire to enter law enforcement. His buddies, Ty and Keith, hadn't either until two years ago. Mortals, magics, and shapeshifters still talked about damn near making the national news. The Great Reveal had followed. Some folks still wanted magics and supernaturals herded into holding areas. "We're like them in so many ways. We love, laugh, cry, and even use their bloody damn technology. We just want what they want. Live our lives in peace." James sighed as he reached the end of the moving walkway. Two small crowds stood in front of the elevators leading to baggage claim. At a trot, he headed down the stairs to the left of the elevators. If he made it to baggage claim before the elevator crowd, he could grab his bag and be at one of the car rental counters, avoiding all the noise, pheromones, and latent magic oozing off some of them. How mortals ignored their abilities was beyond him?

"Siobhan, I'll meet you on parking level two of the short-term lot. It's right across from baggage claim. Did the movers contact you?" Elana glanced at her watch. The moving company had texted her three times yesterday confirming their mid-day arrival today.

"Yes, bright and early too. Five-thirty a.m.! Two blasted texts and three calls."

Elana pressed her lips together trying to suppress her smile. If Siobhan worked last night, she probably had hoped to grab a witch nap, thirty minutes of deep sleep, then head to the airport. "Sorry. I told them to contact you after ten a.m. I'll see you in a few. Crowds thinned out. Should be able to get to baggage claim quicker." Elana disconnected not catching what else Siobhan said. She'd repeat it if she felt the need once they were together in the car.

Partway down the moving walk, Elana snickered. Holiday tunes and Christmas decorations cropped up amongst the remaining fall decorations.

Discounts on Halloween items sat at the front of the shops she passed along with Thanksgiving discounts. The holiday season was in full gear. Many of the passengers passing her carried large shopping bags filled with wrapped gifts. When had the year-end holidays all rolled into one ongoing event? Halloween, then Thanksgiving, and now Solstice. This year was going to turn out different. She had a home, a home where she would spend the holidays. Being home for the holidays meant not worrying about next-door neighbors or whose invitation she'd accept or working the winter interim class schedule. She'd be in charge. The aspect sounded delightful when she voiced it and delicious when she contemplated it.

Rather than wait for the elevator, Elana started down the stairs. Everyone said moving at her age was vital and important. She outpaced most of her coven sisters on their five-mile weekly walk. Keeping active was the central part of her life. Her dog-walking business kept her busy three days a week. The five-mile weekly walk added to her step count, keeping it well over the ten thousand mortal health experts recommended. Her doctor suggested slowing down. Slow what down? Her sixtieth year on earth wasn't a time to slow down. It was a time to live. To be who she wanted to be. To enjoy life and embrace living joyously and with great vigor.

As she reached the bottom of the stairs, Elana slowed her pace. James stood at the car rental counter close to the baggage carousel displaying their flight number. He hadn't reacted as he walked past her on the plane or in the terminal. Why was his being that close bothering her? It wasn't like she was going to grab his ass and say, "Hi, remember me?" She had couth and she wasn't considering taking up with James again. Slowing down more to ogle James's nice ass, muscular build and . . .Elana halted close to the chairs near the baggage carousel. She needed to focus. Not on her memories of James lounging nude on her bed the morning after a night of little sleep and plenty of sexual fun. She turned around, took a deep breath, counted fast to fifty by fives, and exhaled. Her red and golden suitcase slid down the chute onto the carousel, along with her two other bags.

She moved forward, reaching for the handle of her first suitcase. Another passenger reached for the case at the same time. "Excuse me," Elana said, firmly gripping the case's handle. "This is my case."

"Just being helpful, Elana."

Elana didn't need to look up to know who that voice belonged to. James was right beside her. "Thanks. I've got it."

"You probably do. I want to help. Besides, I have a question for you." James stepped back as she hefted the suitcase off the carousel.

"Hold your thought. I'll be with you in a moment." Elana moved to her right, reaching for her second suitcase.

"Just tell me which ones are yours, please." James was shadowing her.

Elana glanced to her left. People were watching them. She could take an assertive stance and draw more attention to them. Or accept James's help and find out what he wanted. "The golden one that passed us. And this one." She pointed to the red case passing in front of them.

James grabbed the case and set it next to her. "I'll get the other one." He trotted around the carousel, picked up the other case, and approached from the opposite side. *He'd recognized her.* Her peace of mind was in pieces as it tried to figure out what he could possibly want.

"Okay, any others?" James set the case next to her other two.

"No. Thank you for helping me." Elana faced James. "Do you have your bags?"

"Yes. By the car rental counter." James moved into her line of vision. "Shall we move before the crowd gets bigger?"

Elana shrugged, pulled out the handle on the case closest to her, and tipped it back on its rear wheels. "My ride is waiting for me."

James leaned in and whispered. "I know. Lance can't pick me up and there's a two-hour wait for a rental car. Lance suggested I snag a ride with you and Siobhan."

Elana gripped her suitcase handle harder. Not back in Cauldron Falls an hour, and already people were trying to set her and James up again?

"How does Lance know Siobhan is picking me up? Someone else could be picking me up." Elana reached for another of her suitcases.

"Siobhan closed the bar early last night stating she had to come pick you up. It's no secret we're here for the holidays." James picked up her other suitcase along with his.

Elana sighed and rolled her eyes skyward, silently asking why Lupa was tossing her and James together. Elana stumbled as a thought crashed through her mind. Last week, she'd talked about wanting to meet a man with several of James's qualities. Lupa, she hadn't said his name.

You thought it. Great, her conscience was getting in on the act. Her thoughts weren't private? *Not from me, darling. After all, I am you. Stop fussing and accept the deities heard your unspoken desire. You want a mate and here he is.*

"Let me call Siobhan and see if she's okay with giving you a ride." Elana quickly uprighted herself, glanced at James who smiled and shrugged. She walked over to a row of chairs near the exit and took out her cell phone. Siobhan answered on the first ring.

"Siobhan, I've got a question. Do you mind giving a friend a ride, too?" Elana glanced at James. He stood far enough away she could talk candidly.

"I've got room for you and James. Who's the friend?" Siobhan yawned. "Sorry. Not a good night's sleep."

"Understood, dear. Not another friend. Just James. How did you know it was him?" Elana clenched the phone tighter in her hand. Had Lance and Siobhan set this up?

"Lance called me a couple of minutes ago. He asked if I would give James a ride to his mom's. I said sure." Siobhan's next statement garbled.

"I didn't hear you." Elana motioned to James. "We'll meet you near the crosswalk to the parking deck for door seven."

"What's up?" James asked, moving closer.

"You've got a ride. We're meeting Siobhan in the parking deck across from our exit door." Elana stuffed her phone back in her tote and grabbed the handles of her suitcases. She and James were back together for the next forty-five minutes to an hour depending on traffic to get James safely to his sister Amelia's place. An hour more with James max. Congenial ride home, sign off with the movers, and the peace and quiet of her own place. Simple and easy, right?

TWO

James pulled his cell phone out of his jacket pocket. Reception at the airport had gone from intermittent to none after they exited the terminal. He hadn't bothered rechecking the phone figuring reception wouldn't improve until they were closer to Amelia's. His phone showed two text messages and a voice mail. Siobhan and Elana were talking as they exited the highway.

The two texts were from Lance. He said he needed to talk with him. Amelia had tried to reach him and got his voice mail. James dialed his voice mail, putting the phone to his ear. He smiled as Elana pointed at the sign across the street from the stoplight.

"Antonio's is still open? Last I heard, he and Martha were retiring to South Carolina." Elana turned partway in her seat.

"They did. His grandson Arturo bought the business. Said why change a good thing. Name and food are well known. Chef Blackstone still works there." Siobhan turned on to Witch's Elm as the light changed. "James, what is Amelia's address?"

James held up a finger. "Change in plans. Amelia is out of town. She forgot to give Lance the key. Not enough room in his studio apartment for me to stay there. Frack, I hope I can find a hotel room."

Siobhan shook her head. "Rooms are all booked up. Holiday high season. Aunt Elana, how about your place? You've got two extra bedrooms."

Before Elana could reply, her phone rang. She looked at the caller id. It was the driver from the moving van. "I need to take this."

"Hi, Gordon. What's up?" Elana blinked, scowled and blinked again as Gordon spoke.

"Got some bad news, Ms. Jones. Truck broke down outside River City near the state border. It's going to take two days to get another truck here. Sorry for the inconvenience. I'll keep you updated as I know more."

"Thanks for the heads up, Gordon. I hope you're all okay. It's not your fault. I'll check with you in a couple days." Elana ended the call after confirming Gordon and the movers were all right and staying with relatives close to where the truck broke down.

"Okay," Siobhan began, slowing for a stoplight. "Guess that means I've got company. Hope you don't mind sharing a room and a bed."

"A bed?" James and Elana said almost simultaneously.

"I can sleep on your couch," Elana said.

"No, Elana. You take the bed. I'm the odd party out. I'll make do with the couch." James patted her shoulder.

Elana fisted part of her jacket in her hand. Brushing James's hand off her shoulder or pulling away was inconsiderate. He wasn't being nice just to do so. What he said was true. *But. . .*Blast her conscience didn't know when to shut up.

Oh, come on, sweetie. It's really you that is thinking this. You know you aren't going to make him sleep on the couch. Especially if Siobhan still has that lumpy piece of crap she had the last time you visited. It's not like you're going to grab each other and do the horizontal bop every night like a hormone-driven, lusty couple. Or is that what you would like to do?

Elana closed her eyes, inhaled slowly, and unfisted her hand. She opened her eyes as Siobhan spoke. "Doubt you'll fit on my loveseat, James. The king-size bed with the pillow top mattress in the guest room is much better."

James chuckled. "Yeah, sleeping like a donut does have its disadvantages." He removed his hand from Elana's shoulder. Had she tensed up while he touched her? Or was he reading more into things? He wasn't sure it was her as he entered the plane. There hadn't been time to put his contacts in this morning. He'd fished his glasses out of his carry-on as he entered the airport. Trotting from security to the gate hadn't left time to find his contacts in his carry-on.

"James," Elana began, turning more in her seat. "I'm sure we can share a bed and behave."

"Okay. I suggest we play it by ear. You know it's a full moon and a Sadie Hawkins one. I am unattached and so are you. Right?" James leaned back in the seat. He knew Elana hadn't had a steady beau in quite a while. He wasn't about to put her through more than a bit of teasing with Siobhan in earshot.

"All right you two, TMI!" Siobhan said in a loud voice. "I don't need this information. My poor mind is reeling."

James laughed harder. "Siobhan, you do blush such a lovely shade of red."

He could see Siobhan watching him in the rearview mirror. She stuck her tongue out and rolled her eyes. "Maybe you want your aunt to blush too."

Elana held up her hand. "James, who are you flirting with? Me or Siobhan?"

"Why you Elana, my dear. You, of course." James puckered his lips and blew a kiss at Elana.

He couldn't see much of her face as she gave him a sideways glance. If he were a betting man, he'd take even odds on Elana trying to ignore and glare at him simultaneously. She knew he knew that look. Five years of dating and another six as neighbors shoved them into the category of exes in so many ways. Ex-lovers, ex-enemies, and ex-exes. That last designation was the one that each of them vigorously denied every time anyone brought it up.

If Elana hadn't insisted on propriety during her tenure at Wichita River University, he would have made his continued interest known. But, Elana had worn propriety like it was some magical underwear she couldn't ever take off. Moving to Magic Mountain had taken his mind off her for a while. Opening his business and traveling had taken him places he would have never seen otherwise. Europe magics and supernaturals loved technology when it worked. Finding a way to circumvent magic's transmissions and getting technology to work had taken trial and error along with much research. Who knew using less magic tempered its transmissions?

"All right," Siobhan said, turning into her condo complex. "I'm calling a truce. I need sleep after a quick snack. Six hours of solid sleep. I don't need suggestions for my subconscious to rake my dreams. Got it?"

"But Siobhan," James began.

"No buts, nors, and ors. I am declaring a truce starting now." Siobhan pulled into a parking place close to the last building in the complex.

"James, I think we've been outvoted." Elana straightened in her seat. "How about toast, scrambled eggs, and chamomile tea? I'll make the eggs. James, I'm sure you can handle making the toast."

"Sounds good to me. I'll shower while you make the food." Siobhan shut off the car. "I'll get you towels and toiletries if you need them beforehand."

James shoved his cell phone into his jeans pocket. Some men would consider themselves lucky. Others would roll their eyes and frown. He knew he had an opportunity to get reacquainted with Elana or let his thoughts die where his imagination wanted to go. When Elana had bent over lifting her suitcase off the baggage claim carousel, he'd gotten a nice view of her pert ass and luscious curves. Model-thin women weren't for him. He liked women who enjoyed life, weren't afraid to admit they were wrong, and knew what they wanted in the bedroom. Well, what they didn't want. He wasn't sure Elana wanted him in hers. At the moment, she didn't have much say on that. Neither did he.

"I'll bring the suitcases up." He unfastened his seatbelt and opened the back passenger door. "I've got my duffle and carryon bag. Elana go on with Siobhan. I'll get yours."

"First," Elana said, getting out of the car. "You need to go up with Siobhan to see which place is hers. Second, I can help with the luggage. Women are not fragile."

Siobhan rapped on the roof of the car. "That's enough. Do you want everyone to hear you? Know you two are sharing a *bed*?" Siobhan stressed bed as she raised her voice.

"Siobhan," Elana scolded, looking over her shoulder. "Please lower your voice."

James edged closer. "You might have folks thinking we'd chose each other already. I got some looking and considering to do. All the ladies might find me the best choice tonight."

Siobhan and Elana faced James. He swallowed hard. Glares and scowls weren't easy to miss. His foot was going to be very soggy if he kept chewing on it at this rate.

"Excuse me, Siobhan," James said, leaning down to pick up his carry-on and duffle in one hand and one of Elana's suitcases in his other. "Lead the way. I'll follow Elana. I'm right behind you."

Elana grabbed her tote and the smaller of her remaining suitcases. "James, let Siobhan carry the one you got. You can take the larger one. Even the load out for you."

Elana moved closer to Siobhan and whispered. "Let 'em think it's the heaviest. If he'd offered to help instead of assuming, I'd get the handle out for him and he could wheel it up to the door."

Siobhan briefly shook her head as she locked the car. Maybe after they ate and slept, things would calm down. At least her neighbors hadn't overheard much, had they? "Please show him. I'd like to get inside without my neighbors gawking and gossiping. Reputations and rumors don't mix well."

Elana grinned. "Well, dear. Look at it this way: maybe someone will be smitten with James tonight. Sadie Hawkins choosing happens tonight."

"Not if I don't open the bar. I can't work if I am sleepwalking. Food and sleep. You two can banter or bicker in your room with the door closed after we eat, okay?" Siobhan didn't wait for an answer. She gripped the handle of Elana's remaining suitcase and walked away wheeling the suitcase beside her.

James moved up beside Elana. "When were you going to tell me they all had wheels?"

"Possibly once we got inside." Elana stepped away, following Siobhan.

James set Elana's suitcase down, pulled out the handle, tipped the case back on its wheels, and followed Siobhan and Elana. Lupa help him. If he were choosing, Elana was the one. Well, knowing the person he was going to spend the next three days and nights with, maybe the next thirty days too—well, at least until next month's Sadie Hawkins full moon wasn't such a bad idea. . . or was it? Their past attempts at matchmaking hadn't turned into more. Why would now be any different?

Because you still want her. Find her attractive. Come on, dude. Stop bsing yourself. Elana didn't steal a piece of your heart. You gave it to her and are glad you did.

Sixty-two years young and his conscience was lecturing him. James picked up his pace. Elana and Siobhan stood at the entrance watching him. He smiled as he got to the door. "Making sure I hadn't left anything in the car. Thanks for waiting for me."

"Wouldn't want you wandering up and down the hall looking for which door you needed to knock on." Elana pulled the door open.

"Name on mailboxes usually takes care of that." James entered the lobby.

"If the names and box numbers corresponded to the condo designations." Siobhan followed him. "But they don't."

James shrugged as Elana glanced at him as she followed Siobhan into the hallway off the entrance. This round Elana scored. The day was young, the night yet to come. With some food and sleep, she better watch out. He was going to be ready for round two. Elana had issued a challenge. He was ready, willing, and able to tackle her and her challenge.

THREE

"Aunt Elana, thanks for cooking breakfast." Siobhan covered her mouth as another yawn overtook her. "I'm heading to bed. You and James are on your own. Please keep your banter at a low decibel level, okay? Meaning my wolf ears don't rouse me trying to make out what's going on. Got it?"

Elana wrapped her arm around Siobhan's shoulders. "My dear, I am sure James and I are going to talk for a bit. He was yawning as we ate too. I am feeling drowsy myself. I can't promise anything. I'll do my best to keep my responses down. It's up to you and your wolf senses to keep curiosity next to nil."

Siobhan laughed. "That's why I wear earplugs most of the time. Once my human and wolf senses are sleeping, my subconscious relaxes."

Siobhan kissed Elana's cheek. "I'm glad you're here. Sleep well. I'm going to turn in."

Elana waited until Siobhan closed her bedroom door before entering the kitchen. She rinsed the last of the dishes, put them in the dishwasher and turned it on. James was already in their room, possibly showering. Lupa, she hoped so. Walking in on him naked—wait, that word had too many sexual connotations. Walking in on him undressing wasn't something she was prepared for. Sleeping with him was certainly something she'd prepared for. Some would look at the two of them and shrug. How could a sixty-plus witch matchmaker and a sixty-plus wolf still have lustiness happen? She knew one thing: her hormones had nudged her twice when Siobhan mentioned James would be sharing a room with her. Elana fanned herself as she entered the short hall leading to the guest room and bath.

"She-wolf lovers and men don't mix. Not a problem for me, cuz I'm a lusty wolf."

Elana clapped her hands over her ears. Goddess, James was caterwauling again. Off-key and loud too. He called it singing. Why did it have to be the ditty he made up about her in college? She'd spent the better part of two semesters denying the lyrics referenced her and James's short hot fling over a full blue moon weekend. If he didn't tone it down, Siobhan would be demanding to know who scored first. And neither of them. . .wait one damn moment! James was naked. Elana fanned herself more. The word was nude. The pictures flashing through her mind could dang well stop. She was not jumping into bed with James.

Oh darling, yes, you are. There's no other place to sleep unless you like a hard cold floor. Come on, admit it. The thought of him a few feet away at best stirs the embers, doesn't it?

"Shut up, psyche." Elana tossed her tote on the bed. Next to it she flung the smallest of her suitcases. She opened it and began taking items out, laying them on the bed next to the case. She wiped her hands on her jeans, walked to the closest dresser and opened a drawer. She quickly shut it. Siobhan should have warned her. Elana pulled the drawer open a bit. She looked down, gulped and closed her eyes. Inside were two boxes of condoms, several adult play toys and a . . . no, her niece couldn't be kinky, could she? Wait, no those had to be Ty's. He forgot them, and Siobhan put them in the drawer for safekeeping, yes? After all police used handcuffs. Not Siobhan. Elana pulled the drawer open more. Two other items caught her attention. . . .A leather quirt and a flogger!

"What's wrong Elana?" James asked from behind her.

Elana slammed the drawer shut and spun around. "Nothing, James. Not a thing..." She moved her lips, but her voice refused to speak. She glanced up and down James's torso like she was seeing him for the first time. He was practically buck na—nude. The word was nude, not naked. James wore only a towel barely wrapped around his waist. And it was slipping off him too damn fast.

"Why did you slam the drawer shut? See a mouse? A snake?" James reached for the drawer knob.

Elana grabbed his wrist. "No snake. No mouse. Nothing in the drawer. Which set of drawers do you want?"

James chuckled. "The ones on the same side I'm sleeping on. Or do you prefer to wrestle for them? You know buck ass naked like we used to do on those cold frisky mornings."

"James, the word is nude, not naked. We never..." Elana stopped speaking as James flung his hand up.

"Darlin' you gotta unknot them bloomers, get into some of those sexy lady panties you used to have me wash and fold. You know come into the now times. Heck, just strip off your clothes and run for the shower. You'll feel better." James grasped the ends of his towel, slowly working it lower off his waist and down off his hips.

"*James*," Elana rasped out, hoping her voice was low enough to not echo. "What are you doing?"

"Getting ready for bed. I'll unpack when we wake up. Some good old bare-assed cuddling just might help relax you. Flesh to flesh. . .What ya say?" James grinned, winked and tugged his towel lower.

Elana grabbed her clothes off the bed, stuffed them back in the suitcase and clicked it shut. She pointed at James. "You keep that towel on. Find your pajamas and get them on, please."

James laughed. "Pajamas? Honey, naked as the day my mother whelped me is how I sleep."

"You seriously expect me to believe you're going to sleep na— I mean nude at your sister's?" Elana set her suitcase on the floor next to her others. She opened another, reached in and pulled something out. She tossed it on the bed next to her tote.

"I brought sleep shorts. If you ask nicely and give me a kiss, I might model them for you." James rewrapped his towel around his waist. He set his duffle on the bed, unzipped it, reached inside and pulled out a pair of shorts with hearts and flowers on them.

"You keep that towel on. I can see those shorts quite good from here." Elana took a pair of slippers out of her tote. "You can put them on after I'm in the bathroom. I'm going to take a quick shower. I hope you can behave unchaperoned."

"I could come with you and wash your back. Keep you company. That way you don't have to worry." James flung the shorts over his shoulder. "I could give you an anatomy lesson too. You know reacquaint you with a certain male body. . .mine."

"James Warren," Elana said, putting her hands on her hips. "I am very familiar with male anatomy. I passed basic biology, thank you. I don't need a refresher course."

James shrugged. "When you're ready, willing and able, honey, so am I." He started to unwrap his towel again. "This towel is damp and chilly. Now either you head for the bathroom or you're going to get an eyeful of this glorious senior body."

Elana gulped, grabbed her slippers and nightgown off the bed. She trotted toward the bathroom, paused at the door and glanced back at James. He stood na—frack, she wasn't fighting it any longer. James was bare-assed naked facing away from her. Praise lupa! She bet he had a hard-on happening too.

Honey, you want him turned on. You're turned on. A little sexual play before sleep might take the starch out of your bloomers and put a glow where you need it.

"Shut up psyche. Nobody asked you." Elana rushed into the bathroom, closing the door quickly behind her. An opinionated conscience, a horny male, and her imagination all running rampant in directions she hadn't prepared. . .

How do you prepare? Get washed and jump in bed with him buck ass naked darling that's how.

Elana tossed her nightgown on the counter, dropped her slippers on the floor, and looked in the mirror. She started to point a finger at the mirror, ready to scold. . .great James had her talking to herself. What next? *Three and four orgasms like before?*

Elana spun around, her back to the mirror, as she stripped off her clothes. Cold showers usually dowsed the urge. Right now, she needed a shower and a gag to shut her blabbermouth psyche and conscience up.

James glanced over his shoulder as he gripped his towel tighter. Elana had snuck a peek before she rushed into the bathroom muttering. Teasing and bantering with her was fun. The more flustered she got, the more upset she appeared to be. That wasn't the result he expected or wanted. Had he pushed things too far? Maybe he needed to apologize. Coming right out and asking her if she desired him would push her further into denial. Her pheromones reached out and blatantly fondled his libido. The heat rising off her ramped his hormones up more than he anticipated.

Last time he was this horny, he'd jacked off three times. Third time the female wolf in question helped him. Not that Elana was going to do that any time soon. James inhaled slowly, counted by twos to sixteen, and exhaled as he tossed the towel over the back of a chair. He pulled a second set of sleep shorts out of his duffle, pulled them on and got in the bed. He laid the pair of shorts he showed Elana on the bed so she wouldn't miss them when she came out of the bathroom. Let her think he'd gotten into bed naked. He'd wait and toss back the covers calling out touché as he did. Would she get the joke? What was it going to take to crack her icy veneer?

Elana turned the shower off. The heat of the shower plus a full stomach relaxed her. As she toweled off, she looked in the mirror. Her breasts sagged some. Her nipples weren't as perky as they once were. She had wrinkles and laugh lines. Her tan had faded even more with the change of weather. Her spring had come and gone not without its pain and joy. Sixty wasn't old. That was for damn sure given the way James was flirting with her. Could she turn off the teacher role she'd worn for so long? If she decided to take James up on his offer, no one else needed to know. Tonight she was lead matchmaker, the head of the group recording the matches Cauldron Falls' unattached women made. If no one chose James, maybe she could convince him to stay longer and . . .Elana winked at her reflection. After she and James got some sleep, he best look out. A few kisses and cuddles might liven things up. Liven things up alright. . .could they keep the noise down until Siobhan woke up? Until they tired each other out? Had either of them learned how to orgasm quietly?

Elana hung her towel up, slipped her feet into her slippers and tossed her nightgown over her shoulder. James was probably naked, waiting to flash her. A bit of show and ogle was good at any age. She was ready, willing, and very able to return the favor. As she reached for the bathroom doorknob, she inhaled and exhaled slowly. Being naked was one thing. She and James had visited the naturalist colony near campus frequently. Being vulnerable might be easy if you had something to hide behind like clothes. Naked and vulnerable—together, that was stepping outside comfort zones she hadn't breached in quite a few decades. Maybe it was time to jump over them and...Frack, she could keep on philosophizing or open the damn door and surprise herself and James.

Well honey, are you going to do it or not? Her psyche just had to have the last word!

FOUR

One soft snore followed by another sounded as Elana entered the bedroom. James lay on his back, covered up to his waist. The shorts he'd teased her with were close to his feet on top of the sheet and blanket. Had he fallen asleep naked? She started to reach toward the covers, curiosity driving her motives. Inches from clasping the sheet and peeking underneath, she stopped. James stirred, pulling the covers higher as he turned over. She grabbed the shorts as they started to fall. James didn't stir. Another soft snore sounded. She looked down at the shorts she held, trying to focus on anything but images of crawling into bed naked with James dancing through her mind.

Elana drew her hand back, moving away from the bed simultaneously. She stared at the floor beyond her hand. Ripples of shade and sun danced across the floor stopping near her. Lupa, was this a signal? A sign from the powers-that-be to let things be?

As she looked up, a sunbeam illuminated the shorts. All right, she got it. Put the shorts down and get into bed. She opened her mouth, ready to voice her question aloud. She glanced over her shoulder. Was her blasted psyche at it again?

Elana walked over to the dresser, tossed the shorts on top of it, gave the drawer she opened earlier a wide berth as she made her way back toward James's side of the bed. His glasses lay on his pillow next to him. She picked them up and laid them on the nightstand. As she rounded the bed, she tossed her nightgown next to James's shorts. Let him deal with his imagination when he woke up. Finding her naked in bed with him might ignite something. She hoped it wasn't yelps and disbelief.

She closed the blinds, set the alarm on her phone, and pulled the covers over her. As her eyes closed and sleep claimed her, Elana sent a prayer of thanks to the powers that be. She didn't know what tonight or the future would hold. For now, she was safe. Safe and at a place that might be home.

Six Hours Later

Siobhan rolled over and looked at her clock. Her alarm would go off in fifteen minutes. She took out one earplug, cocked her head toward the bedroom door. Quiet, silence and lush quiet greeted her. She took out the other earplug and placed them in the dish on her nightstand next to the clock. Twice as she slept, she dreamt about Ty and his interest declaration. Their thirty-day match was almost over. Neither of them had said a word about continuing it. He'd laughed the night she'd called out his name as both of their names moved to the top of the list to go into the matchmakers' choice drawing. Lupa, she got off easy that time. They weren't due to declare intent for another thirty days. Solstice permitted last month's matches exemption from declaring if they were going for another thirty or casting their name into the drawing again. Ty's kinky cousin Trina's gift had opened up possibilities. There were other ways of being dominant and submissive without including pain. Though it was so close to pleasure.

She tossed back the covers, turned off the alarm, and stood up. There was time to clean up her vibrator and herself before she dressed. Wet, soap, rinse. Then food. She needed to make a grocery run. She hoped Aunt Elana and James liked chili, cheese and crackers. Otherwise, they'd have to wait until they got to the bar to grab a quick bite. Or as Ty often said, "Depends on where you're biting." Hmmm, he could bite and nibble in the best sensuous places. Her clit and nipples could stop swelling. Taking a cold shower didn't have much appeal.

Ten minutes later, Siobhan exited the shower. She toweled dried her hair, brushed it, and braided it. Ty had asked her to not braid it or put it in a ponytail. He could ask all he wanted. He was damn lucky she'd let it grow out. Short, sassy and easy was her preferred style. Yeah, each of them had flexed some for the other. Like Ty letting her pick up the check for some of their public dates. Being a feminist had its strong points. Then there were times when allowing the guy to be the lead was nice. Very nice. Ty treated her real good on those nights. Multiple orgasms and blissed-out sleepovers definitely chalked up points on those nights.

She tossed jeans and underwear on the bed. As she walked to the closet, she glanced out the window. Sunset wasn't for another hour. The colors illuminating parts of the sky foretold of the storm approaching. Dark clouds checkered the sky, blocking out patches of light. Behind the clouds, bursts of white, golden yellows and blue outlined the change creeping in, ready to reach down with its icy fingers. Frost had come earlier than expected. Northern Montana might see snow in time for Solstice.

Siobhan pulled her long-sleeved flannel shirt out of the closet. Sadie's embroidered in gold arcing letters over a full moon stood out against the shirt's dark blue color. She'd promised Earl Thomas when she bought the bar the name wouldn't change. Had Earl known when he named the bar after his dear departed mother that it would become the focal point of the Sadie Hawkins full moon festivities? Siobhan often wondered if Sadie Thomas' spirit visited each full moon. Some talked about the white-haired lady who watched as matches were recorded. If others skeptical of any magic or supernatural influences scoffed, they kept their thoughts to themselves.

As she dressed, Siobhan reviewed the list of items she needed to take to the bar. Magnolia—aka Maggie—Nickerson and her cadre of apprentices and staff would show up around eight. Right as the moon rose. If her gaggle of squawking females shut up, introductions might happen around eight-fifteen, allowing Elana time to set up her table along with the Sisterhood of Three. Maggie boasted she was Cauldron Falls' premier matchmaker. Disastrous matchmaker was more like it. More thirty days and done than with the elder matchmakers. Competition kept things interesting. But vying for the handsomest and richest amongst mortals, magics and supernaturals. . .what happened to good old attraction? I wanna jump your bones lust? Maybe Ty put it best when he said a full moon brings out the loons. Lupa, was Cauldron Falls attracting outliers?

"Louie will be on hand for the festivities too. Watered down beer, lots of steak tartare, garlic cured venison and plenty of breath mints." Siobhan grinned as she picked up the aluminum baseball bat she kept beside her bed for self-defense. Louie's twin, Louie 2, would rest on the bar close to her until the crowd thinned out. Ty, Lance, and Keith were assigned to the bar for the night.

Siobhan tied her hikers and stood. Were Aunt Elana and James awake? There was time to eat before they left for the bar. Once there, things would demand her attention until closing. Eating needed focus before she went into work mode. That meant prepping food now. As she entered the hall separating the bedrooms from the main living area, she stopped, cocking her head from side to side. Quiet. . . were they still asleep?

James brushed his lips across Elana's. She pulled back, blinking. Her eyes flashed open.

"James, what are you. . ." Elana didn't say more. She looked down. Down to where his hand rested on her shoulder. She glanced up. James's gaze met hers. He smiled.

"I'm giving you a wake-up kiss." James rolled on his side. "Your alarm went off twice."

Elana pulled the sheet higher. "Thanks. What time is it?"

"Time to get up since your alarm went off." He chuckled. "Why is your nightgown on the dresser?"

"Maybe I wore something else to bed?" Elana tried to stuff the sheet under her arms as she attempted to sit up.

"You can wrap the sheet around you all you want. I know you're naked." James tossed the covers off him and stood. "Give me a moment and I'll be naked, too."

He clasped the waistband of the shorts he wore. His gaze still on Elana.

"Wait." Elana pointed at him. "You had those on all the time?"

"Yes. Why do you. . ." His grin deepened. "Oh, you thought you'd get one up on me."

"Perhaps I decided to take you up on your unspoken offer." Elana shook her head as she continued. "Hand me my nightgown please."

"No." James shoved his shorts off his hips and over his legs, letting go of them until they pooled at his feet. He kicked them aside as he stepped out of them. He walked around the foot of the bed until he was in Elana's sight. "Now we're both naked. How about a couple of moments cuddling?"

"James, are you serious?" Elana turned, holding the sheet in place with both hands. "I'm over the shock effect."

James closed the space between them, squatted down and laid his hands on the bed. One on each side of her hips. "Shock wasn't my intent. Flirting. Banter. And at one moment, one-upmanship. You played along."

He watched Elana's breasts rise as she inhaled. She caught one of her lips between her teeth, slightly worrying it. She might not remember he knew what was going through her mind. He did. Elana knew he was on to something. Would she admit it? Or avoid it?

"I did play along. I won't deny I find you attractive. You get my hormones going. Your masculine wolfish scent reaches out and zings me in all the right places like you used to tell me about my witchy scent." Elana leaned back on her hands.

"What you gonna do about it?" James started to rise.

Elana held her hand out. "Take you up on your offer? Nude cuddles. We used to be able to do that. Nothing more."

James straightened, clasping Elana's hand. "Offer accepted. Cuddling is a good thing. We don't have time for more if we wanted more."

Elana laughed as she let go of the sheet and scooted back making room for James to sit beside her. "Truth is, Siobhan might knock and if we didn't answer, she'd open the door to see if we were still asleep or what."

James picked up the sheet and sat beside Elana. "Yeah, we wouldn't want to scar Siobhan's virginal images of us nude. You know, old and clothed in bed."

Elana drew up her knees and rolled onto her side. "She'd be yelling TMI for sure on that one. There's that damn drawer too."

James lay on his side, pulling the sheet over them. "You never said what's in the drawer."

"Remember Sasha and Edward from our junior year at Shamrock Falls University?" Elana moved closer to James.

"The two that Elliot and Marybeth hung out with until they went to one of their house parties?" James laid his arm across Elana's waist.

"Yes. Rumors were they were kinky. Leather connected community members." Elana combed her fingers through James's hair.

"Oh, those two. Yes, the whips and quirts were everywhere to quote Elliot and Marybeth." James grinned. "That's what's in the drawer?"

"Sasha and Edward made leather gear for the kink community. Never knew if they were very kinky themselves. Didn't need to know. Didn't ask." Elana pressed her lips to James's. She pulled back, continuing the conversation. "As to the drawer, yes. And a pair of handcuffs and condoms."

James pulled Elana closer to him. "Should we set them out on the dresser in flung places, plus a few condom packets torn open?"

Elana pressed her lips together hoping to contain her mirth. James rested his forehead against hers, winked and puckered his lips. She looped an arm around his neck as she pressed her lips to James's.

Out in the hallway, Siobhan fanned herself. Frack, she'd forgotten about the drawer. Ty hadn't slept over in three weeks. Damn, Lance for forgetting his handcuffs last time he and Ty came over for dinner. Lupa, her aunt and James were smoldering when she closed the door. Who needed TMI of the verbal kind? She'd just witnessed TMI of the visual kind. Her aunt and James buck assed naked, making out! Siobhan fanned herself as she trotted down the hall away from the guest room.

FIVE

James shrugged and went back to eating when Siobhan looked at him. Elana glanced at Siobhan. Siobhan hadn't said much. It wasn't like her to be standoffish and quiet.

"Siobhan, is something wrong?" Elana laid her spoon on the table next to her empty bowl.

"No." Siobhan shook her head, looked up, flashed a grin and went back to eating.

"You've been very quiet. Are you sure there's nothing wrong?" Elana asked, picking up the last of her cheese and crackers.

"Very sure. Just thinking about tonight." Siobhan put her spoon in her bowl. She ate her remaining cracker and cheese in two bites. "Maggie and her cohorts are gonna stir up shit. She thinks her matches are the best. Her bevy of trainees can't get a scrying mirror to glow dimly."

James leaned close to Elana. "Go with the flow. I'll tell you what I think is up when we get our stuff from our room."

Elana nodded, picking up on Siobhan's comment. "Maggie's great-greats were Cauldron Falls' matchmakers for years. They were the first. Course if you don't procreate, you don't get future matchmakers. If your procreates is all males. . .well, I'll leave it at that."

James coughed. "Are you saying males are second class?"

Elana gawked at James. "Did I say that? Matchmaker magic is a female magic gene to my knowledge. You took Basic Magic Biology one-o-one and passed it, right?"

"Sure did. Maybe there's a male matchmaker out there. Maybe several." James put his dishes in the sink. He turned on the hot water, stoppered the sink, and added dish detergent. "Just like we males can cook, do dishes, and keep house. Oh, yeah raise youngins, too."

Elana set her dishes on the counter. She took the dishtowel off the rack close to the sink. "Good to know. Though I doubt you got procreating and diaper duty on your mind at your age."

"Ah, sexual fun is good at any age. Kids. . .no that duty is for those Siobhan's age." James ran rinse water into the second sink. "Right Siobhan?"

"I've got stuff to do before we leave." Siobhan put her dishes on the counter and almost trotted out of the kitchen.

"What's with her?" Elana asked, rinsing the bowl James handed her.

"Remember when I said I thought I heard the door click shut when we were cuddling and fondling?" James put another bowl in the rinse water.

"Yeah. . ." Elana set the dried bowl down. "Ah, shit! She saw us?

"Possibly." James held out another rinsed bowl to Elana. "Nothing we can do about it. She knew that could happen without knocking first. Not that we would have heard her."

Elana took the bowl. "Yeah I did have my mouth and hands full for quite a few moments."

James grinned. "Yep and I returned the favor too. You taste divine, darlin'."

Elana glanced toward the kitchen doorway. Siobhan wasn't in sight. Hopefully, she wasn't within earshot either.

Siobhan fanned herself as she entered her bedroom. Lupa, heat rolled off her aunt and James like two teen shifters ready for their first full moon wild morph. Her libido had picked up on their sexual attraction from the moment they started bantering in the car. Pheromones rolled off each of them, threatening to swamp anyone within reach. Her hormones were on high alert thanks to the full moon rising and her time of month. Her menses was late. When she and Ty examined the condom, the tear was near the top. The reservoir tip held the bulk of Ty's ejaculation. The rest smeared the inside of the condom. Had he overflowed the condom? Part of his ejaculate seeped out onto her as he withdrew? Crap, neither she nor Ty needed a forced marriage. Neither of them wanted an embittered marriage like either of their parents had.

She wiped her face with a cool cloth. Her menses was late again. Blast, irregular menses cycles. If she didn't start cramping soon, there was a pregnancy test in her and Ty's future. Siobhan wrapped her arms around her middle and hugged herself as tight as she could. There were so many unknowns happening tonight. She hated uncertainty. She took a deep breath, held it and slowly exhaled. She wasn't getting any younger. Maybe there was a brighter, happier side to this. She'd deal with that if and when the pregnancy test showed she needed to. Right now, it was time to focus on work and keeping the festivities from going out of control.

She sat on the bed and picked up the list she'd jotted down before sleeping. Louie II lay on the bed next to her work duffle. Extra bandages, antibacterial ointment and pepper spray along with her apron and hooded sweatshirt were in the duffle. If snow fell before morning, she'd need the sweatshirt. She stashed extra menses supplies in the duffle before zipping it shut. One last glance at the list showed everything checked off. Twenty minutes until they needed to leave. She hoped Maggie behaved herself. Knocking a matchmaker upside the head wasn't going to gain her points. Siobhan leaned back, closed her eyes, and muttered a short incantation prayer, hoping that magic deities were on duty tonight. None of them needed anyone unlocking Hades for grins and giggles.

Elana hung up the damp dishtowel. "Tonight is going to be unique."

"How so?" James asked, putting the last of the dried dishes and utensils away.

"I'm officially matchmaking. Doing it without watching, noting and ready to step in is different. My focus is on the magic. The people choosing. Reading auras, demeanor, and non-verbals all at the same time. My third eye is going to be very busy tonight." Elana laid her hand on James's shoulder. "I'm glad you're going to be there. Knowing that calms me. Thanks for cuddling earlier."

James kissed her cheek as he slipped an arm around her waist. "What if I get chosen? What if she doesn't want to share?"

"James, are you ready to pack up and go with another woman you don't know?"

"Not happening anytime soon. Get to know her and see what happens. I ain't agreeing to more until Amelia gets back and I know I got a place to stay if I get picked." James winked at her. "Besides, I can always say no too."

Elana laughed. "Yes, and push yourself right back to the top of the list, too."

'I'll play the age card if I have to. We, seniors, get a say in our choosing. I am not going to be some horny female's sex toy. Used, worn out and tossed aside. No, not going there." James moved away.

Elana nodded. "Let's go get our stuff. We need to get going. Siobhan said it takes forty minutes to get to the bar."

James took hold of her hand and squeezed it. "If Maggie starts crap, my money's on you and the elder matchmakers. Respect, dignity and trust are important when making matches. Tonight is also a celebration of your homecoming. I'm here if and when you need me."

Elana nodded and let go of James's hand. If she were choosing tonight, she'd choose James. Matchmakers didn't make full moon choices. Custom and tradition required their full attention during matchmaking. Usually their choice matches were made after the full moon passed.

Siobhan entered the front room as she and James exited their room. "Ready to go?" she asked, slinging the duffle bag onto her shoulder and carrying Louie II in her other hand.

"Sure are." James held out his hand. "Anything I can carry out to the car for you?"

Siobhan shook her head. "Thanks. I've got it. I'm hoping tonight is quiet and uneventful."

"A Sadie Hawkins full moon quiet?" Elana asked as she zipped up her coat.

"Just Cauldron Falls folks. No rival packs. No horny unmannered teens. Or morphing until they get outside or home. I don't need extra mess to clean up. One late morning closing is one too many. I need my sleep. Like ten hours' worth!" Siobhan keyed in the alarm code before she closed the door. "Kristy from Delancey's is bringing by three dozen fresh baked donuts and breakfast croissants on her way home around three a.m."

"Oh lord, stuffed stomach stupor after eating those." James got in the back seat. "Knowing I get Delancey's for breakfast....oh yeah! Mint tea, fresh donuts, and a couple of breakfast croissants stuffed with ham and cheddar cheese...I'm pretty sure I am turning down my pheromones. I ain't missing those goodies!"

"James, I am not nursemaiding you through a stomach ache!" Elana fastened her seatbelt and closed the car door.

"I eat that much and I hibernate, love. Even my cock will snore. You don't have to worry." James reached forward and caressed Elana's cheek.

"Do *you two* think *you* can behave tonight?" Siobhan put the car into gear. "You know, act mature?"

Elana turned in her seat, facing Siobhan. "Siobhan, we are acting mature. When you get to be our age, you've learned sex is awesome stuff. Nothing to be negative about. Positivity is priority."

Siobhan glared at her, shook her head, and went back to focusing on her driving. Elana clasped James's hand and let go. Decorum was expected. Sensitivity needed and being herself off the job. . .well, it was time to start living life how she wanted to.

"Siobhan, do you need to talk about what's bothering you? Don't tell me there's nothing. I can read your aura from a mile off. It's not its usual periwinkle and golden hue." Elana laid her hands on her thighs. Siobhan couldn't hide her anger or upset well. She oozed with affection and contentment most of the time. Prior to her latent limited magic traits developing, she'd shunned groups. The funk she gave off would send even the horniest male shifter running for the woods. As much as she wanted to give Siobhan a hug, Elana respected Siobhan's right to not talk about it.

As she slowed for a stop light, Siobhan spoke. "If I say anything, it's confidential. Between you, me and James. Okay?'

James leaned forward. "Siobhan honey, if I need to put my fingers in my ears. I can do so and sing off-key quietly."

Siobhan giggled. "You don't need to do that. I don't need either of you trying to fix things. If I need that kind of help, believe me, I'll ask *both of you* for it. Right now I need to talk."

"Sure. Go ahead." Elana turned more in her seat so she could see Siobhan easier. "I promise to listen. Offer my opinion and not expect you to do what *I* think is best."

"Me too," James said.

Siobhan glanced at her aunt and James as the light changed. "I might be pregnant."

"Might be pregnant?" James shot his hand forward. "Before you say more Elana, I am repeating what Siobhan said."

"Go on Siobhan. We're listening." Elana clasped James's hand and let go.

"My menses is possibly three months late. I'm moody like it was going to start. Cramped a bit. Then nothing. Thought I was going through an irregular cycle again." Siobhan wiped a tear away and shook her head. "I probably need to get a pregnancy test."

"Oh, sweetie," Elana said, laying her hand on Siobhan's arm. "I'm not going to ask how this happened. James and I both know how."

Siobhan laughed. "I wish I could tell you time, place and position."

"TMI!" James called out.

"Got ya!" Siobhan replied. "I suspect a condom blowout."

"Have you talked to Ty about this?" Elana asked.

"How can you be sure Ty is the one?" Siobhan slowed to turn into the parking lot for the bar.

"If it isn't Ty, okay. If you are pregnant, you're going to need to tell the father." Elana straightened in her seat as Siobhan parked.

"Maybe I will. Maybe I won't. Right now, I've got a business to run. Tomorrow is time enough to get the test and find out. I need to be in the here and now tonight." Siobhan unfastened her seatbelt. She gripped James and her aunt's hands. Her emotions had run from giddy happiness to scared depression. Raising a child wasn't easy with two parents present. One-parent parenting took lots of patience and skill. Lupa, her mother had taught her that. The few times her piss ant sire had shown, he wanted to show her off like a prized trophy. So what if she was one of the few witchy shape shifter mixed bloods with some of the old world magic traits. Maybe her child would be mortal, non-magical. There was a chance that could happen. Wouldn't that pluck a few nerves, particularly her piss ant sire's?

SIX

Siobhan opened the driver's side door. She dabbed her cheeks with the sleeve of her coat. Mood swings were a usual part of her pre-menses cycles. Where had this swing between elation and tears come from? "I gotta pull myself together. I'm the assertive barkeep. I take no prisoners. Well, except maybe cute ones."

James chuckled. "Siobhan, you're doing okay. Once you get to work, you'll be all right. Focus is what you need. Know Elana and I are here if you need us. You're not alone. As to the cute ones, some prisoners might be nice."

Siobhan smiled as she turned toward James. "Thanks James. You and Aunt Elana didn't expect this as part of your homecoming."

"Surrogate parents is part of being part of the pack. Part of the community. The line about needing a village to raise a child, take care of a family, and each other is true. It applies whether you're a magic, shape shifter, or mortal." Elana came up beside James. "Everyone needs a second mom or second grandma. Even a second poppa or second grandpap."

"True," James said, slipping his arm around Siobhan's shoulders, giving her a quick squeeze. "We'll work this out together. Let's get inside and get set up. That moon is rising."

As they neared the bar's entrance, Siobhan pointed to a car close to the door. "Maggie is here already. She's probably chattering someone's ear off asking where I am."

"*Pink Car*? Does it have a dimmer switch?" James blinked and shielded his eyes. "There's enough glitter on those door signs to illuminate the interior of a house when a bright light hits them."

Elana snickered. "They say part of advertising is catching your clients' attention. Standing out in the crowd."

"That ain't gonna get noticed if you're too busy puking and looking away. Damn, Maggie must have attention issues." James continued to shield his eyes as he made his way past the car.

Siobhan wiped her cheeks again. The tears flowed this time from laughter. "James, I do hope you're not going to walk in and puke on Maggie."

James clapped his hand over his mouth, leaned against the doorframe as he turned, pointing at Elana and Siobhan. Peals of laughter slipped out from behind his hand. Several moments passed as the three tried to compose themselves. Each time they glanced at the car, more laughter erupted.

James wiped his eyes and held up his hand as he spoke. "Praise deities, no one walked by us. They would have thought we'd lost it for sure. The owner and the two old cronies have gone way around the bend. Call the nut squad to come and get em."

"Come on let's go in and see what Maggie's stirred up." Siobhan grabbed hold of the door handle. "Last time, she had two lines going as she took names and put them in a hat."

"Not very magical about choosing matches that way." James moved up next to Siobhan. "More like taking bets on odds or evens. Nothing unusual about that. Straight-out math. Either you get a name you want or you don't."

Elana patted James's shoulder. "The magic is in choosing the right name. That is why we elders allow people to choose three on the list. Male chooses three females and stands in the moonlight with each. The one's aura they can see is usually their match."

"Yeah, works for magics and preternaturals 'cuz we got the power. It's in our nature to see auras. What about mortals?" James stepped back as Siobhan opened the door more.

"That is where we matchmakers come in. Crystal choices leave imprints of a person's energy. Mortals choose a crystal chip and hold it for thirty to forty seconds. They place it on the white sheet of paper on the table under the full moon's light. The magic, shifter or mortal making the choice points to the one that is drawing them." Elana followed Siobhan and James into the bar. "It's not ultra-scientific nor highly magical. It works and that is the important part."

Siobhan turned as they got a bit further into the bar. "Maggie has her back to us. Now would be a good time for me to go in the back and check with Chef. I'm sure she's given him an earful or two."

"Go on Siobhan." Elana hugged her. "James and I will handle the Pink cyclone and her fawning wannabes."

"Yep, we promise to behave a bit. Not promising if it's a bit bad or a bit good. Mischief isn't at the top of the list." James grinned and winked.

"Let's call it damage control, and beyond that I don't need to know." Siobhan smiled as she walked away.

James moved closer to Elana. "Who else is supposed to be here?"

"Naomi, Tara, and Zelda. Cauldron Falls' three oldest matchmakers. The Sisterhood of Three." Elana unzipped her coat. "We graduated together. They went on to other enclaves needing matchmakers until the Great Reveal. Then coming home made sense."

"You didn't." James took off his jacket, flinging it over his shoulder. "What changed your mind?"

"Wichita River's offer. A chance to teach what I knew to potential magics and help mortals understand us. It worked out great. When Wichita integrated magics, shifters and mortals, my class load expanded. Supernatural history, crystal magic and matchmaking needed a professor. And shall we say the rest added up to my retirement." Elana walked to the coat rack close to a table with a sign on it reading Sisterhood of Three.

James hung his coat on the rack next to Elana's. Where were the other matchmakers?

Siobhan slipped out of her jacket as she entered her office. Two stacks of paper sat middle of her desk. She slowly inhaled and exhaled. The two piles of bills were just as she'd left them after closing last night. The week's receipts weren't enough to cover all the bills. Losing money wasn't easy. Closing the bar and going out of business wasn't an answer. Many saw Sadie's as one of Cauldron Falls' cornerstones. A place where they could come, gather with friends, sometimes their families and have fun. If she was pregnant, she'd be working less. Hiring someone who understood the business, the business atmosphere, and what Sadie's meant to Cauldron Falls wasn't going to be easy or something she had much time for.

She pulled open the bottom drawer of the desk, dropped her fanny pack inside along with her jacket, and locked the drawer. Her focus was here at work, not on what might be. When Ty came in tonight, she would make time to talk with him. Actually, take a dinner break. Thirty minutes to discuss hey I might be pregnant and what are we going to do about it. Siobhan sighed as she tied her apron around her waist. Nothing might come of the discussion. Shrinking the elephant figment down to a mouse was worth the thirty-minute surprise guess what conversation.

Chef walked up to her as she exited the office. "Evening Siobhan. Have you looked over tonight's menu?"

Siobhan grinned. "Pretty much what we serve every full moon. Steak tartare, low alcohol beer and wine, a few specials and our regular menu of burgers, pot roast and stew."

"It's tonight's specials I'm asking about." Chef held out the menu.

Siobhan slid her finger partway down the menu. She looked up at Chef. He nodded. "New Orleans Crème Brule with Ceylon True Cinnamon. Six-ounce Angus steak cooked to order, double baked loaded baked potatoes, zucchini and broccoli florets with light buttery cheese sauce and baked from scratch yeast rolls."

"Is there more?" Her mind already calculating the cost of ingredients.

"One other. Stuffed chicken and portobello alfredo with fettuccini, garlic rolls, tossed salad and New York Style Peppermint Cheesecake with optional hot fudge sauce." Chef pointed to the bottom of the menu. "The items can be ordered a la carte. This provides options which may get us more orders for the specials."

Siobhan exhaled slowly. "Okay, we push the specials and a la carte, then."

Chef nodded. "The Sisterhood of Three and Maggie covered part of the acquisition costs for the specials' ingredients. Besides, Pierre and I wanted to have a wonderful meal available for your aunt's welcome home meal."

"Thank you, Chef. I appreciate your and Pierre's sentiments. Lance's uncle James will enjoy either meal too. You've got two orders for sure." Siobhan handed the menu to Chef.

"One last thing, Siobhan. We have reservations for fifty-plus people tonight. Many are holiday diners. Others are looking for matches." Chef smiled, adding. "Looks like the moon will be closer and brighter tonight. That may bring in extra walk-in traffic."

"We can handle it. Lance, Keith and Ty are on security duty. I got Louie II with me. You got the tasers back here. I guess we are going with Bluetooth earpieces tonight." Siobhan started back toward her office.

"Two steps ahead of you on that." Chef held out his hand palm up with a Bluetooth earpiece in it. "Charged and ready to go. Gregorio is manning the front door, checking people in as they arrive. Capacity limits will be enforced for safety measures."

"Thank you, Chef. I appreciate you overseeing this. I hope tonight is quiet and good matches are made." Siobhan put the earpiece in her ear and adjusted the volume.

"My pleasure, Siobhan. Partners work together to make their business a success. Pierre, you and I are going to make it through the holidays."

Siobhan nodded as Chef walked away. Partnerships and matches required working together for a mutual outcome. Would Maggie and her bevy of assistants and trainees understand that? Or was chaos waiting for the right moment to pounce?

SEVEN

Elana turned as James moved up beside her. "Zelda, Tara, and Naomi should be here setting up."

"I think they are. Away from the maddening crowd." James pointed to a section of tables toward the middle of the dining area. "Been a bit since I saw Zelda. I think that's her waving and coming toward us."

"You're correct. Glad your glasses give you eagle eye vision." Elana nudged James as she moved past him.

James chuckled. "Darlin' as long as I can see you clearly and pick you out of the crowd, my specs are awesome."

"Elana, glad you are here." Zelda moved forward, her arms open, ready to hug her.

Elana embraced Zelda. Power whelped up, ready to snare her into its depth. Elana pulled back. "Are you shielding?"

"Yes. Been a rough day at the hospital. Several births, colds, and flu. A couple of Willow Creek centenarians passed away last week. Two nurses related to the family are back off bereavement." Zelda wrapped her arms around herself. "Emotions are running high. Solstice full moon is adding to it."

"Elana, glad you are here." Tara patted Zelda's shoulder. "Tonight you are the record scribe. You keep shielding. Your aura brightens some each time you let go of the urge to take on others' feelings."

"Thanks, Tara. Being an empath isn't easy." Zelda clasped Elana's hand, squeezed it and let go. "I'm going to see if Siobhan has any of the wine I like in stock."

Tara faced Elana. "Naomi is cleansing the crystal chips. We were able to get them directly from the warehouse. Little or no magic has touched them."

"Good. I wondered if we were going to have to limit the number of matches because of that. How many do we anticipate tonight?"

"Depends on who they choose for their matchmaker. The glam and glitter of the younger generation or the way traditional matchmaking magic works. You go with your heart, gut and psyche." Tara glanced over her shoulder. "Maggie is going to try to outdo us."

"Let her. People make choices. They have free will. Mortals are going to see things one way. Magics and shifters another. The beauty is mutual respect. And some healthy competition." Elana smiled.

Tara leaned closer. "Don't be surprised if Maggie challenges your unmatched status."

"*My what*?" Elana stared at Tara. "No one has ever challenged me on that."

"Maggie purports matchmakers' magic doesn't work if they're not matched." Tara shrugged as she continued. "Not that her matches are record-making. Longest one lasted two weeks."

Elana snorted. "If she publicly challenges me, I'll have to. . ."

"Have to what?" Tara patted her shoulder. "Make a match choice? No biggie. We do have quite a few older gents signed up for tonight."

"Yeah, me included." James winked as he walked by carrying a stack of chairs and following Zelda.

Elana rolled her eyes, clenched her fists, and let out a deep sigh. Apprentices had challenged her. Students had challenged her. Never a wannabe. Much less one that drew attention to herself with cars and signs that screamed notice me, I want your attention. Elana pressed her thumbs against each fingertip as she counted to a thousand by twos and fives. Anger had no place in the matchmaking process. Chaos created more confusion and less matches than if everyone grabbed who got their hormones juicy and flowing. Maggie may have her matchmaking license, but. . .that was a massive rock in the flow. . .it sounded like her success was more in the minus column than in the plus. Elana glanced at James. He waved. Was Lupa and deities at it again? Trying to set them up?

Sweetums, you know you want it. So why you fighting it?

Now her conscience was joining in again.

Oh, stop fussing. Let loose and snag the man. He's ready, willing and certainly able. You found that out earlier.

Elana pressed her lips tighter together. Muttering to herself and fussing at her psyche and conscience wasn't going to happen. Especially when Maggie with the fakest Cheshire cat smile stalked across the dining area toward her. Oh, if she thought she was going to pull a considerable knockout punch. . .she had another thing coming. Matchmaker magic worked both ways. Point out bad matches and the fakes too.

Elana held out her hand, her finest sweetest fake smile illuminating her face. "Maggie, how good to meet you. May the full moon enlighten and show us the way. Gods and Goddesses bless us all. Luna clara nos dirige nos magicae hac nocte."

Maggie wiped her hand on her skirt. "Nice to meet you too, Elana. I've heard a lot about you and the Sisterhood of Three."

Elana pressed her lips tighter together as Maggie's palm slid across hers. Heat burned across her palm, inching its way up to her wrist. Elana pumped her hand up and down, quickly letting go. Cold iced its way across her face and hand. Maggie stared at her, grinning as if she'd pulled off a fast one. What she'd done was show how inept her magic was. The air sizzled briefly and returned to the moderate internal temperature of the bar. Maggie knew some magic and tried to ooze it like a net waiting to snare her prey within its trap. Elana stepped back, putting her hands behind her back, flexing them. This one used her sleight of hand like a clumsy mortal magician. Lupa and Goddess help her. Maggie needed training. Guidance in how beguiling magic could be. How to use the traits she possessed and understand that leading didn't mean bespelling others or using parlor magic to stand out. Elana started to turn as Maggie continued speaking. "Elana, you're still single? Why? A matchmaker who can't find her own match?"

Elana turned slowly back toward Maggie, her fists clenched. Never had anyone cast doubt on her matchmaker magic. Magic students understood that matchmaker magic didn't mean they could make their own match. Some needed assistance, like what Zelda, Tara and Naomi did. They pooled their magic, amplifying its effect. Matchmaking involved the heart, attraction and purpose. A few mortals referred to it as getting set up on a blind date. Sometimes the crystals chose for the matchmaker without her knowledge. Deities and the One added their guidance and knowledge.

Elana flexed her hands, slowly exhaled and responded. "My match was teaching. Enlightening mortals and other magics, along with supernaturals, how magic works, especially matchmaking magic. Matters of the heart aren't simple. There are emotions, attraction, purpose and connection. I understand very few of your matches have reached their first or second anniversary much less an engagement party or nuptials. In fact, aren't you single? Why haven't you found your match? Matchmaker can't gin up her own match?"

"We're talking about you. Not me." Maggie pointed at her.

"Put your finger down, Maggie Lawson," James called out. "Your elders knew magic is a living force. It can and often defies a set description or attempt to make it conform to specific rules. You might have learned if you bothered to finish your internship and family magic history class."

"Shut up, James. No one gave you permission to intervene." Maggie raised her hand as she turned toward James.

"Raise your hand to an elder and banished ye shall be. Respect and dignity fill this one that seeks to instill fear and chaos." Zelda stepped between James and Maggie. "The Sisterhood and those present will testify at your banishing trial if you keep it up. You overstep your boundaries. Stand down or pack up and leave. Luna reigns tonight. Her magic protects all who respect and use it wisely."

Siobhan, holding Louie II, moved up beside Zelda, Chef and Pierre, along with Tara and Naomi. "Maggie, I've tolerated you and your wannabees because I treat everyone with dignity and respect. You keep provoking stuff and threatening my aunt and James, you are expelled. Out of business here at Sadie's. There's enough business tonight for you and your group as well as the Sisterhood of Three. Are you standing down or are you leaving?"

Anna, one of Maggie's trainees, spoke up. "We want to learn from the elderesses. The Sisterhood of Three and Eldress Jones. My mother was a matchmaker until she retired. She taught practical magic, crystal magic, and healing to those who wished to learn. Maggie Lawson, repetition is awesome until it becomes boredom. There is more to magic than just putting names in a hat and shuffling them around. Tonight we all learn. Please make peace and embrace change."

Maggie backed away muttering. As she got close to James, he patted her arm saying, "Elana's got a match, me. We chose each other privately. Our heart magic began before tonight. Luna's magic reignited the passion, connection and caring with Lupa's help. Younger magics' approaches help instill change and respect for magic, connection and emotion. Good luck with your matchmaking tonight."

"Yeah, right. Thanks." Maggie mumbled, walking away.

James glanced to where Elana stood. She watched Maggie make her way back across the dining area. Elana and Maggie's silhouettes were outlined in red and yellow. Aura colors from his experience that didn't signify peace was at hand. He'd lay even odds on Maggie stirring up more manure before the evening was out. He rolled his eyes heavenward, silently hoping she left magic out of it. Witch's honor prohibited Elana, Zelda, Tara, and Naomi from physically hurting her. That left lots of other areas wide open.

EIGHT

Siobhan wiped the bar down. Ty had come in a few minutes early. He'd waved and disappeared from sight. Lance and Keith congregated close to the entrance. People flowed in behind them like waves crashing upon the shore. She'd lost count after the twenty-fifth person entered. Pierre as he filled glasses, said his tally was close to seventy. More came through the door. None exited. Siobhan tossed the wet towel in the hamper under the bar. As she washed her hands, she peered out over the crowd looking toward the back where she'd last caught a glimpse of Ty. He and James were helping Elana finish setting up. Maggie had staked out her area with the help of her wannabes close to middle of the dining area. James had caught on and helped open the skylight blinds completely.

As the moon rose, its light shined down on both matchmaking sections. She had to make the official welcome announcement accompanied by the rules reminder and ensure everyone had food as they waited their turn to meet with the matchmakers. Sadie's was damn near filled to capacity. Siobhan looked up, catching sight of the moon as she muttered a short prayer. "No argument from me on your blessings. Just not fights and chaos. Matches yes. Anger, hate and discord not tonight, please."

Chef set the first tray of hors d'oeuvres on the bar. "Glad you changed up the raw meat to cooked. Too many shifters get a snoot full and want to rumble. Too many present tonight for that. We got cheese, crackers, sushi, and shrimp. Next tray will have cold cuts, mini baguettes and dips to add to their first round."

"Split things between both trays. Put them out on the buffet. Lance and Keith can keep an eye on that. If you see Ty, send him over to me, please." Siobhan wiped her sweaty palms on her jeans.

"Noted. I saw him close to James and Elana as I exited the kitchen. Here comes Pierre. He looks like he forgot to sugar the lemon he sucked. Last time I saw that look, some debutante pinched him on the ass and claimed he was hers for the night." Chef picked up one tray.

"Was that before or after he pinched her back and said her ass was so flabby no one could get even a decent handful?" Siobhan grinned.

Chef leaned close as he rounded the bar. "He read her her beads that night, too. Before and after. The infamous 'Thank you, not fucking you, and leave my ass alone. Only my partner gets to bruise and kiss em to make them better.'"

Siobhan clapped her hand over her mouth. She pressed her lips tighter together. Snorts and muffled eeps of laughter sounded. Chef grinned, nodded and started off across the dining area. He paused long enough to share a steamy, passionate French kiss with Pierre beneath the full moonlight streaming in through the skylight.

Siobhan leaned on the bar. Sadie's legal capacity was one hundred and fifty folks. Or as the capacity sign read, people, animals and/or a combination thereof. The line below that read, 'That includes magics!' Her aura reading abilities scrambled as the crowd grew and intermixed mingling began. She glanced down. "How do I tell Ty about. . ."

"Tell me about what?" Ty asked, sitting down on the bar stool in front of her.

"Come on back into the office with me. Less noise and possible eavesdropping." Siobhan walked to the end of the bar and paused. Ty moved up beside her.

"This must be important. You don't leave the front while the bar is open." Ty pushed open the kitchen door, waiting for Siobhan to go first.

"It could be." Siobhan didn't say more until she and Ty were outside her office. "Did you get your dinner? Do you want anything while we talk?"

Ty walked over to where Chef kept a buffet ready for the staff. He filled a plate with tossed salad, a chicken breast, a burger and two cookies. As he set the plate on the tray, he grabbed a set of napkin-wrapped utensils and a bottle of water. "Are you eating?"

Siobhan nodded. "My plate is already in my office. Grab me a bottle of water, please."

Ty set the second bottle of water next to his on the tray. "Anything else?"

Siobhan pulled a napkin out of the dispenser close to the tray of cookies and pastries. She wrapped the napkin around three large sugar cookies and entered her office.

Ty put the tray on the desk next to Siobhan's plate. He uncapped the water bottles and sat in the chair in front of the desk. Siobhan closed the door before she sat down opposite him behind her desk.

Siobhan sipped her water twice. She had thirty minutes to eat and find out how Ty felt about possibly becoming a dad. She took the napkin off her utensils and lay it on her lap. Ty was cutting up his burger and chicken, mixing them in with his salad. Siobhan speared a hunk of chicken with her fork, looked at Ty and asked, "How do you feel about kids?"

Ty gulped water and swallowed twice, praying he didn't spit all over himself and the desk. He wiped his mouth, stared at Siobhan, and laid his fork down. "That's an off-the-wall question. Why do you ask?"

Siobhan held up a finger. She chewed her food and swallowed. "Remember when we talked about birth control and making sure there weren't any surprises?"

"Yeah. This is about the torn condom." Ty tossed a piece of chicken in his mouth and quickly chewed.

"It is. I'm tired a lot more. My breasts and nipples are tender and my sweet tooth is running rampant." Siobhan popped a piece of sugar cookie in her mouth and chewed.

Ty leaned back in his chair. "Have you seen a doctor? Taken a pregnancy test? How late are you?"

"No test. No doc yet. My menses have been irregular last six months. Could be more. I haven't checked the calendar for the date of my last menses. Busy working, preparing for my aunt's arrival and keeping up with holidays." Siobhan ate several bites of chicken, waiting for Ty's response. She wasn't sure she could look at the calendar for an exact count on how late she might be. Pregnant and. . .Goddess, did the fear ever stop? Why was she scared of a possible pregnancy? It wasn't like health care was at a distance. Cauldron Falls' medical facilities were top-notch. Best in the supernatural realm and even understood mortal health needs. Siobhan took a deep breath and laid her fork down. "Ty, are you thinking about proposing? Cuz you have to?"

Ty leaned forward, holding out his hand. "Well tonight is Sadie Hawkins Full Moon. It's not unusual for couples to declare their intent."

"Ty Cobblestone, I won't marry you because you think you gotta. Our child deserves a set of loving parents. Not an arranged hitch because a condom broke!"

"First, no broke condom was arranged. Second, you don't know if you're gonna pop something out nine months hence. So what are you complaining about?" Ty grabbed his fork, poked his salad, and stuffed his mouth. Damn, he hadn't planned on arguing with Siobhan. He wanted tonight to be about deepening what they had. Plans for the future. Make a verbal commitment to each other. What that entailed, he hadn't figured out. If Siobhan was pregnant, he wasn't walking away. His parents had stuck it out because they thought they had to. What a fucking failure that was. They fought and never bothered to soothe him and his siblings post loud caustic arguments. His child was not going through that. Marriage might not be the expedient answer. Any kid of his was going to know his father loved him or her and would be there for them.

Ty finished chewing and swallowed. He drank part of his water and put the bottle down. "Siobhan, I don't want to argue with you. My comeback was low and uncalled for. I'm sorry."

Siobhan nodded. She kept eating, not responding. Ty exhaled and resumed eating. Maybe this was what they needed. Time to let the heated exchange dissipate and things cool down.

Siobhan chewed, swallowed and ate more. Part of her wanted to spew angst-filled remarks. She wasn't letting fear drive. Scared and unsure wasn't good either. Right now, she needed composure. Ty was trying to communicate. She caught him off-guard as much as a possible pregnancy had her. Dreams of holding her child filled her sleep. Daydreams of this too. Was her body telling her what she suspected was true?

"Ty," she began, setting her plate aside. "I think we're both in shock. Dealing with something we thought we had control of."

"You can say that again. Two dominants trying to figure how to give to the other and deal with our submissive side, aka parenting and how we feel about each other." Ty finished his salad and water. "What I'm trying to say Siobhan, is I'm here for you and if you're pregnant, our child."

Siobhan pushed her last sugar cookie to the middle of the desk. "Neither of us likes getting caught off-guard. We're planners. Even our sex is almost planned out. Maybe we need to let go and deal with the unknown."

Ty nodded. "Split the cookie with you."

Siobhan grinned. "Sure. How about we get a pregnancy test from the pharmacy and meet at your place? I think we want to know the result before we tell others."

"I agree." Ty broke the cookie in half. "We're in this together. Do your aunt and James know?"

Siobhan smiled. "Yes, I told them. They've got our backs. Let's meet around eleven for breakfast. I'll cook."

"Okay." Ty checked his watch. "Ten minutes to spare. Wow, that's the fastest argument and make up we've ever had."

Siobhan laughed. "Probably not our last either." She laid her hand on the desk, palm up. Ty laid his hand on top of hers, palm down. Warmth touched each of them.

Ty squeezed her hand and let go. "You're not alone in this. I'm here for you. Doctor's appointments. Testing. Wherever you need me. Whenever you need me."

Siobhan sighed. "Thanks. Hopefully, your work won't interfere with things."

"We'll take things one step at a time. If I have to put in for paternal leave, I do it." Ty stood, dusting his uniform pants off. "We're going to work this out."

Siobhan placed their dishes on the tray. "I don't want either of us promising things we can't keep. Let's take this one step at a time. Test results first. Then we talk more, maybe plan, okay?"

Ty nodded. Neither of them could plan for the unknown. He vowed after discovering his parents' backstory, none of his kids were going through constantly wondering if they were loved and wanted. From what little Siobhan had said, she'd possibly been through similar. Tomorrow would yield answers. Were they ready for whatever the test result was?

Elana motioned James to her. "Have you seen Siobhan and Ty?"

"Not since they both went into the kitchen. Why?" James glanced around the dining area. A few customers sat at the bar, talking and drinking. Others mingled in groups around the perimeter of the matchmaking area.

"Maggie is watching the door like she's waiting to pounce. One of her former pupils told Tara that Maggie is prone to gossiping." Elana took her nameplate and matchmaker ledger book out of her tote. She placed both on the table closest to her.

"Gossiping how?" James shrugged as Elana gawked at him. "Explain please."

"Sorry. Maggie makes statements like she's foreseen something and adds bits and pieces hoping to enhance the story." Elana looked to where Maggie stood, watching her and James. She glanced toward the kitchen door twice as she wrote on a pad.

James moved closer to Elana. "Seems like there's prognostication coming. Do I need a trash can for the manure or pith helmet and flack jacket?"

Elana glanced at Maggie. "From her scribbling and look, possibly both and extra like hip-high boots and a pressure hose. My prediction is there is going to be a lot of manure and grandstanding going down."

NINE

Maggie walked to the middle of the dining area, calling out as she did. "Everyone, can I have your attention, please."

Elana scanned the room, focusing her attention toward the kitchen. Was someone alerting Siobhan?

"I heard Pierre mutter something about needing backup." James clasped Elana's hand. "I saw him enter the kitchen."

"Yes," Elana began as Siobhan and Ty, followed by Chef and Pierre, exited the kitchen. "Crowd control is here. I'm joining Zelda, Tara, and Naomi upfront." Elana squeezed James's hand and let go.

"You'll be fine." James brushed his lips on hers. Adding as he pulled back, "I'm here if any of you need me. I got clean-up patrol ready to commence. Twit thinks she is going to burst your balloon. It's hers full of manure and bad karma that's going to burst if she ain't careful."

"Let's hear her out. She's got a right to say what she wrote down. Keeping the flood from overflowing her mouth will be the tricky part." Elana moved up by Tara, Naomi and Zelda.

Maggie ran her finger down her pad, nodding as she looked back up. The crowd watched her, waiting for her to speak. She inhaled, smiling. Elana, The Sisterhood of Three, Siobhan and her student defectors thought they had silenced her. Won the battle. The skirmish wasn't over. The fight had barely begun. She stepped into the area illuminated by the moonbeam shining down through the skylight portal.

"The One, Luna and the Deities revealed to me important information about certain people here tonight." Maggie held up her pad. "I wrote the revelation down as it came to me."

Siobhan stepped into the moonlit circle. "I don't believe you. Circle wasn't called and sanctified. Premonitions and revelations come within the circle and with witnesses."

"You were not here. You can't challenge me." Maggie rocked back on her heels, gloating.

"I can challenge you. I've been present all along. Spill your so-called revelations." Elana stood next to Siobhan.

Maggie pointed to Elana. "You cannot participate in tonight's matchmaking. You aren't matched. Deities and Luna refuse to accept your presence."

"You lie, Maggie," James called out, moving up next to Elana taking her hand. "We made our match choice privately. Elana has a match, me!"

Siobhan pointed at Maggie. "Apologize to my aunt and James if you want to stay. Otherwise you are banished."

"Silence," a male voice called out from the back of the crowd. "The Matchmakers Counsel decides banishments."

A tall male with auburn shoulder-length hair moved to the front of the crowd. "I speak as the Counsel's representative. Maggie Nickerson, you will hold your tongue. Elana Jones, do you publicly accept James Warren as your match choice for the next thirty days?"

Maggie pointed to the male speaker. "Matchmaker Counsel members are only female. There are *no* male matchmakers."

"You are out of order. You do not know all. Your name is spoken with mistrust and loathing by many who complained about your fees and matchmaking attempts. I am Caleb Morningstar, elder leader of the male matchmakers. Males do possess the matchmaking magic gene. We are an elite group." Caleb walked through the moonlit circle until he stood toe-to-toe with Maggie. "Respect your elders and the ways or admit your hoaxer ways."

"I will not. I am a matchmaker licensed and bred. I have the gene." Maggie tipped her head back until her gaze met Caleb's.

"Hear the counsel's decree." Caleb laid his hands on Maggie's shoulders. "You are under my watch and chaperoning for the next thirty days."

"I'm what? House arrest?" Maggie dropped her pad, clenched her fist and drew it back.

"I didn't say you were staying with me, but if you persist. . ." Caleb lowered his hands. "We are matched per council decree. You are permitted to use your magic under supervision. Now are you ready to proceed with tonight's matchmaking or do I escort you home to pack and move into my home?"

"Not over your bold crass body am I going anywhere with you." Maggie stepped back. Caleb moved forward.

"Are you defying the Counsel's decree? The Counsel?" Caleb stopped as he reached the edge of the circle's illumination. "Luna, the One and the deities hear and see what you are doing. Do you tempt fate?"

Elana held up her and James's clasped hands. "I accept James as my Sadie Hawkins Full Moon match." She faced James. "Do you?"

James stepped into the circle, raising his arm as he backed up until he was center of the circle, moonlight pouring over him. "Is there more you wish to say?"

Elana closed the space between them until they stood tight to each other. "I declare and accept this match. I abide by the matchmaker magic rule set forth by the One, Luna and the Deities. Do you?"

"You give no time limit. You are asking for none." James raised their clasped hands above their heads.

"This I swear be true. This match lasts until we both are done with it." Elana kissed James and pulled back.

"So it is spoken. So I do agree. This match lasts until we both are done with it." James lowered their arms. "Our match is declared as ancient matchmaking law decrees in accordance with the rituals set forth by the One, Luna and the Deities."

Elana asked as she and James faced Maggie and Caleb, "Who else did your revelation include?"

Maggie shook her head. "I don't have my pad. I don't remember."

Caleb bent down, picked the pad up, looked at it and smiled. "It says you agree to a double money-back refund if any of the matches you make tonight don't last out their thirty-day period."

"You lie." Maggie gasped. "That isn't what I wrote down. It says Siobhan and Ty are engaged because Siobhan is pregnant!"

Caleb held the pad up. "There is nothing legible on this pad. You made all of it up. One more reason you are under my watch."

"Just because you can't read my notes doesn't mean I made things up." Maggie grabbed for the pad. Caleb held it up, out of her reach.

"The truth comes from those you claim your revelations are about. I ask them if any of this is truth." Caleb walked over to Siobhan and Ty. "You are Siobhan and Ty, correct?"

Siobhan and Ty nodded. Caleb showed them the pad. "If you can make out any of this, please explain. You are under oath to answer truthfully."

Ty took the pad. " By Luna, the one and the Deities, I answer truthfully. There's a word here and there that might mean something to anyone. Siobhan and I aren't engaged. As to pregnant, I'm not."

Laughter rolled through the crowd. Caleb nodded. "Thank you, Ty."

Ty handed the pad to Siobhan. Siobhan looked down at the pad, at Ty, and handed the pad to Caleb. "Engaged is what might happen tonight if a couple of prior matches decide to declare them. Ty answered about him and I. Pregnant? I'll have to take a test to answer that one."

"So you might be pregnant," Maggie challenged.

"Silence, Maggie." Caleb held up his hand. "I'm asking the questions."

Maggie dropped into the chair closest to her. She folded her arms tightly across her chest.

"Siobhan, you under oath. Are you pregnant?" Caleb lowered his hand.

"I am guided to tell the truth by Luna, the One and the Deities. I can't answer if I am or not unless I take a pregnancy test. And that would be between Ty and me unless we decided to make it public, right?"

"Yes, privacy is respected. Maggie has pushed proprieties boundaries tonight." Caleb faced Maggie. "I rule this way."

Maggie stood, looking down as Caleb continued speaking. "There are gray areas in what is going on. Rivalry is not good. Competitive is accepted as business needs prompt healthy commerce. . ." Caleb's voice trailed off. Maggie looked up.

"Maggie, you are under my watch. Prepare for close chaperoning for an unspecified period to be determined by the Counsel. You may conduct business tonight under supervision and with Siobhan, Ty, and the others say."

"Frack, I'm *not* a child." Maggie turned around.

"*No*, you're not. That's what makes chaperoning you that much more enjoyable." Caleb cupped Maggie's cheek. A low *wow* rippled through the crowd.

"I didn't give you permission to touch me." Maggie kicked out at Caleb, shoving his arm away.

"No, you didn't. Siobhan, Ty, Elana and James didn't give you permission to touch them with your envy and jealousy. Yet you did. Understand why this is not acting in good matchmaking magic protocol. Rules and regulations exist because magic is a natural force that can beguile and deceive if one does not consciously use it wisely." Caleb stepped away from Maggie. "You've learned your first relesson in Magic one-oh-one."

"Yeah, right." Maggie started walking away.

"Maggie, tempting fate isn't a good idea. Remember you're packing up and coming with me starting tonight." Caleb walked away in the opposite direction.

TEN

Maggie stopped close to the table with her ledger and the hats on it. She hoped to be tossing names into the hats as people came up requesting matches. Rivalry her ass. She'd had little or no competition until the seniors came requesting matches. "How am I supposed to get two stubborn stuck in their ways old goats to take a chance on each other?"

"The same way James and I did. You allow them to make a choice. Not just a random pull from a hat full of names. Love, joy and reception come alive when two people connect. If you've never experienced that, no wonder you are tossing magic out in bursts, hoping it sticks to some of those yearning to make connections." Elana held out her hand.

"Why are you offering me your hand?" Maggie looked down and back up at Elana.

"Because this old female goat knows what it's like to forgive and make peace. I went through rough times learning about my magic abilities and lineage. History hasn't been kind to our ancestors. A lot was taught and memorized to keep the oral history and traditions going." Elana started to lower her hand.

Maggie thrust her hand forward. "I'll shake. I'll keep the peace as long as there's mutual respect."

Elana pressed her lips together. Retorts and frustration weren't going to keep the peace. Caleb had passed behind Maggie twice since she approached her. Caleb would report what he witnessed. The Counsel would know what happened tonight, good or bad.

"Fair enough." Elana clasped Maggie's hand and shook. Heat followed by cold rushed across her palm. As Elana drew her hand back, she watched Maggie. Maggie scanned the crowd, looking twice over her shoulder back toward the corner tables.

"We've got matches to make. Let's get started." Maggie faced the crowd.

Elana moved up beside Maggie. "Ladies and Gentlemen, the moon is full. Before Luna waxes and wanes, the One is nigh, and the Deities are ready to hear our heartfelt requests, let the match choices begin. You may choose from myself and the Sisterhood of Three to assist you with your matchmaking or Maggie and her assistants."

"Tonight, I am doing things differently. If you are mortal and want a mortal match, you can choose from the eligible mortals present. Same-sex is welcomed. Know that if you are open to hearing your heart, listening to the still small voice within and your own personal magic, choose three you feel drawn to and make a choice." Maggie sat down at her table. Two of her assistants joined her.

Elana faced Tara, Naomi and Zelda. "Are the crystals ready?"

"Yes. Last night, I dreamed we passed the crystals out as we took names. We asked those who chose us to exchange crystals with the one they felt drawn to." Zelda held out the clear crystal bowl full of colored crystal chips. "Naomi, will you take them to the circle's center and invoke Luna's blessing?"

"I ask you to join me in invoking Luna's blessing. The One visited my dreams last night. They spoke of unity in a time of unrest. My gut says this is the time." Naomi touched the bowl. "Vibrant colors of the heart are ready to burst forth. Blue, violet and mauve outline the bowl."

Elana, Tara, and Zelda entered the edge of the moonlit circle closest to them. Each cupped the bowl with splayed fingers until their hands touched, encircling the bowl as they held it aloft, invoking Luna's blessing together.

They spoke in unison. "Luna bless us and those gathered with us tonight. Imbue your magic and wisdom into the hearts and minds of those seeking to make a match. Empower these crystals and our hearts with your magic and insight. Luna, the One and Deities, bless us with your presence and endow us with your magic and knowledge. Luna, the One and Deities be praised."

As they lowered the bowl, Zelda drew her hands back. "Luna and the One whispered in my ear."

Tara laid her hand on Zelda's shoulder. "I hope it was encouragement, my dear."

Zelda shrugged. "I heard sorrow and pain are parts of life. You've had both. Breathe deep, for joy shall be yours tonight."

Naomi smiled as she turned toward the table. "You best put your name in the ledger. Hawke Cranston is on the list of men seeking to make a match."

"Hawke? He and I haven't spoken in almost six years. Why would he be interested in me?" Zelda sat in the chair next to Elana.

"Why did James choose me? Or were we chosen by Luna and the One?" Elana opened her ledger and held a pen out to Zelda. "Zelda, why not give it a try?"

"Hawke and I didn't part on the best of terms." Zelda reached for the pen. "He wanted a commitment before he left for an overseas work assignment."

Naomi placed the bowl on the table close to the ledger book and pen. "I don't know the details. He asks about you every time I run into him. I say give him another chance. If he doesn't agree to a match with you, there's other men available."

"Zelda, life hands us spur-of-the-moment choices and options. Luna is handing you a choice and option together. Ask Hawke. You won't know unless you ask. Sometimes it takes trusting you and your heart." Elana turned the ledger book around.

Zelda glanced over to where a group of older gentlemen stood talking. Toward the back of the group, a taller male stood. His black hair, salted with white, bobbed as he animatedly talked with the person next to him. Hawke stood out in a crowd. His six-three height and early greying hair won him the nickname after winning the broad jump and pole vault events at a high school track meet. Commentators remarked how he looked like a bird of prey swooping through the air as he competed. Hawke had captured her attention from the first moment he had smiled and winked at her as they crossed paths changing classes in junior high. Their on-again, off-again attempts at dating had tossed them to the wind as their families moved around. Six years ago, Cauldron Falls brought them together as Hawke visited his family before moving overseas. Would he give them another chance? Not picking up where they left off before. Starting with the here and now, focusing on getting acquainted and see what sparked between them.

Zelda faced Elana. "Yes, I am going to ask. Hawke can say no. There are others that interest me. I ask to be in the latter group unless Hawke signs the ledger earlier."

Elana pointed to the bottom of the second page. "Sign here. We'll see how many come before you. Remember to focus on the crystal color your heart draws you to. If Hawke pulls the same color, you ask. If he pulls differently, he gets to ask the one he's drawn to."

Zelda nodded, quickly signing her name. Luna and the One's magic were flowing thickly around the room. Zelda murmured a prayer as she finished signing that Luna and the One would point her to her heart's desire.

Siobhan walked over to the table where her aunt sat. "Aunt Elana, are you ready to go? Begin taking clients?"

"Yes. Is Maggie ready?"

"As ready as she's going to be once she's out of the bathroom. Caleb chuckled as she tried to sneak past him. From where he's sitting, there's no getting past him." Siobhan turned, walked to the center of the room standing directly mid-circle, bathed in moonlight.

"Tonight, Sadie's welcomes all Sadie Hawkins Full Moon participants. The women present will go first. Those who have not chosen their match will have a second chance after the men make their choices. Remember the match you make may be the one you make for life. Good luck everyone," Siobhan announced in a loud voice.

Maggie glanced around the dining area. Caleb hadn't moved from his seat. Ty sat next to him as the two talked. Caleb glanced back toward the hallway leading to the bathrooms. No man had ever bested her. No man dared dominate her. She flexed her hands and rubbed them on her skirt. If he thought she was going home with him tonight he had a surprise coming.

Maggie walked past Caleb. Her posture ramrod stiff. Caleb leaned closer to Ty. "That one is going to be a battle of wills. It's not going to be an easy thirty days."

Ty smiled. "Cousin, I know you can do it. You took on the matchmakers' counsel and won the first male apprenticeship with them. I'm sure you'll figure something out."

"True. Does Siobhan know about your hybrid heritage? Your magic traits?" Caleb stood as he spoke. "I think I have a matchmaker trying to ignore me."

Ty rose. "Any magic I got is minimal. Siobhan and I have a connection. Let's say we're feeling each other out and leave it at that. Good luck with Maggie."

"Thanks, I'm sure I'm gonna need it," Caleb said, walking toward where Maggie sat with her apprentice assistants.

Ty shook his head as he turned around. Full moon magic didn't mess around. Luna opened the way for hearts and minds to hear each other. Two months ago, Siobhan had chosen him on the spur of the moment. He seconded her choice within moments of her announcement. Their initial loose and easy agreement might be changing. Was he ready for that? He glanced up as he walked around the edge of the moonlit circle. The outline of what many referred to as the face of the moon greeted him. He stopped, stared and looked away. Had a planet thousands of miles away winked at him?

ELEVEN

James leaned against the bar, nursing his second beer. Siobhan and Ty sat at the opposite end of the bar talking quietly. The two lines of women grew shorter as each signed their chosen matchmaker's ledger. Maggie stood up from time to time checking where Caleb was. Other than the few moments when he used the restroom, he stayed within Maggie's field of vision. James set his almost empty beer bottle on the bar. Food call would happen soon. The group of men gathered toward the front half of the dining area formed a semi-circle around the outer perimeter of the matchmaking circle. Hawke and several others stood near the front of the semi-circle. Food call would permit mingling before the women started declaring their choices.

"Long night," Caleb muttered, walking up to the bar. "Tension is lessening."

"Yes," James replied. "Women are pretty evenly divided between who they want as their matchmaker."

"Power balance is good to a point. I hope Maggie understands choice." Caleb sat on the barstool next to him. "I could use a drink."

James chuckled. "Well, you got to keep your wits about you. I imagine one shot won't mess you up. I hear Siobhan has some potent twelve-year-old scotch."

Caleb nodded. "A dram in a mug of hot chocolate would be nice. Sugar to offset the alcohol and not enough kick to fog my brain."

"Let me see what I can do about that for you." James laid his hand on Caleb's shoulder. "You keep watching for both of us for a couple moments, okay?"

Caleb grinned. "You're on. And ask Siobhan if she can make my burger a double. We shape shifter magic hybrids need to keep our strength up if you know what I mean."

James walked away laughing. He stopped as he reached Siobhan and Ty. James leaned close to Ty. "Caleb asked for a double burger and a hot chocolate with a shot of the *real good* stuff Siobhan keeps beneath the bar."

"*The good stuff?*" Ty set his coffee mug down. "Siobhan, you been holding out on me?"

"Depends on what you call holding out." Siobhan reached under the bar. "Private stash isn't for public ogling. It's for leisure sipping. Slow and easy leisure sipping."

Ty reached for the bottle Siobhan set on the bar.

"You can look. No touching. That is the last bottle of the last batch Holcomb Parks distilled at Blue Ridge Distillery." Siobhan set a shot glass on the bar. "James, are you joining the tasting?"

"No thanks. Two beers are my limit tonight." James perched on the barstool close to the end of the bar.

"Ty?" Siobhan put a second shot glass on the bar.

Ty pointed to the shot glass closest to him. "Not more than a sip. I'm on duty."

Siobhan set a two-ounce measuring cup on the bar. "How much did Caleb say he wanted?"

"A dram. It's about three-quarters of an ounce." James moved both shot glasses closer to Siobhan. "A splash in one glass. The other three-quarters empty as my great granny used to say."

Siobhan uncapped the scotch, filled the measure to the one-ounce line, and set the bottle down. She picked up the scotch bottle cap, filled it from the measure and emptied it into the shot glass. "Ty, you ready?"

"I'll chase my taste with the rest of my coffee." Ty reached for the shot glass closest to him. "Here's to the unknown."

Ty held the shot glass to his nose, sniffed and shook his head. "If the taste is as potent as the smell, damn that is going to kick."

Siobhan smiled. "First sip or two, it sure does. That's why scotch and whisky are sipping liquors. Most alcohol is."

Ty saluted Siobhan and James with the shot glass, sipped and sputtered. He grabbed his coffee mug and downed a third of the remaining coffee. "Damn, it do gotta kick."

"Yup. Once I thought I could handle that stuff. Tossed back two shots back to back. Next I knew I was looking up at the ceiling wondering how I ended up on the floor." James stood. "I'll let Caleb know you're getting his order ready."

"Hang on James. I've got to put Caleb's order in." Siobhan set two bottles of water on the bar. She pushed one toward Ty. "Cleanse your mouth with this."

James sat on the stool near Ty as Siobhan entered the kitchen. "How you and Siobhan doing tonight?"

Ty uncapped the bottle of water, drank a third, and set it on the bar. "We've talked some. Some decisions can't be made until we know more. Appreciate you and Elana backing us up."

"We'll do what we can to help. Extended family is a blessing." James glanced toward the kitchen door. "Siobhan and Elana's family can be mulish and stubborn."

Ty laughed. "Oh yeah, I found that out firsthand. Siobhan threatened to deck me first time I treated her like a fragile woman."

"Fragile? Elana? Siobhan? Not those two. They are practical, willing to pitch in and help. Opinionated and stand their ground? Oh, yeah." James stood as the kitchen door opened. Siobhan held the door open. Pierre exited first, carrying a tray full of steaming burgers and buns. Chef followed, pushing a two-tiered cart with several covered food trays.

"Caleb's order is cooking. Thanks for making sure Ty didn't fall off his stool." Siobhan patted Ty's shoulder as she walked by.

"Good sense of humor too." James grinned as he turned. Caleb stood near Maggie saying something. Maggie wasn't backing down. Neither was Caleb.

"I'm not going home with you tonight or any night." Maggie moved to the side, ready to step around Caleb.

"I'm going home with you then. We can go by my place in the morning to get my stuff." Caleb held his arms out. "See darlin', I'm not letting you out of my sight."

"Like hell you're not." Maggie drew her fist back.

"Strike me not. I'm a council elder. You're letting your anger rule you. Step out of it. See the opportunity present."

"What opportunity?" Maggie folded her arms tightly across her chest.

"You can choose me as your match. I can choose you. Or. . ." Caleb let his voice trail off.

"Or what?" Maggie stared at him like she hoped to turn him to stone. Wasn't happening.

"We could choose each other and let everyone think the challenge is on. Which it is. But it takes their mind off you being reprimanded."

"Gee, thanks. You're so sure I need this reprimanding." Maggie dropped her hand.

"Softening the rough edges never hurts. Though I understand pain is so close to pleasure. Are you that kinky?"

Maggie opened her mouth, quickly closed it and opened it again. She pointed at Caleb. "*Kinky?* Blessed Luna, no! If you are, you best find someone that enjoys that pain and wants your painful touch."

"Maggie, before you say more, know this. I don't enjoy pain. Matchmakers bring joy. We embody choice, kindness, joy and love. Matches are meant to bring joy. Do all choices work out? No. We aren't forced like our ancestors into arranged marriages that were for gain, position or lineage continuance." Caleb turned, stepping back until he stood next to Maggie. He pointed to the crowded dining area where couples mingled. "This is what we matchmakers represent. Putting names into a hat and randomly drawing them out gives some choice. Some hope and dismay when things work out. Why not let hearts, emotions and attraction honestly take part in the choice?"

"Because people make the wrong choice. They don't see what and how the match can help them." Maggie sighed, turning away.

Caleb grabbed Maggie's hand. "Many do see how a match can help them. They understand making choices comes with risks. They want the joy, the kindness, and the love they know can come from a match. Wisely chosen and with trial and error are all parts of living. What scared you away from embracing life?"

"None of your damn business." Maggie tried to pull away.

"Oh, but it is. See you're my chosen match for the next thirty days. Maybe it's time to show you just how much you attract me." Caleb tugged Maggie to him. He slipped an arm around her waist, stopping her from falling tightly against him. He cupped her cheek, leaned closer, and brushed his lips over hers. "I'm here by choice. The council wanted to send another. See, I've been watching you for some time. You turn me on. I'm a lover, not a fuck 'em and leave 'em heartbreaker. I hope our match works out."

Maggie pulled back, rubbing her lips together. "*Right*. I've got matches to record and a business to run. Later."

Caleb let go of her hand. She looked down, back up at Caleb and shook her head. She'd run into stubborn, foolish males before. Ones who thought they could top her because they were male. Drunk on their own testosterone and over-inflated ego. She walked two steps away, hesitated, glanced back to where Caleb stood nodding. . .he blew her a kiss. Maggie swallowed hard. Why were her nipples tightening and her conscience urging her to turn back around and kiss Caleb?

Caleb smiled as Maggie walked away. The bursts of heat sparking off her as their lips met said more than their verbal cat-and-mouse banter. Strong-willed had its vulnerability points. He knew that one firsthand. He'd learned about his the hard way. Flexing and knowing how to bend like the willow in the wind, no one taught him. Fights, bruises, and the harsh reality that making your own choices didn't always mean you won. Rumors of Maggie going it alone, disowned by her family from time to time, and the ever-changing world demanding you fit in circulated in the whispered gossip groups within the matchmaking council. Like attracted like, right? There was enough different about them that those sparks might be waiting to ignite as well.

TWELVE

Siobhan rapped on the table next to her. Chattering ceased. She stepped forward. "Food is served. You have ninety minutes to mingle and eat. After you've eaten, find a seat at the tables marked with the crystal color you've chosen. Chosen matches sit together. The matchmaker assigned to your group will record your match. Those left will have a second chance to choose. This continues until all are matched. Pairings of more than two are permitted. Same-sex matches are welcome too."

"What if the person we're drawn to has a different colored crystal?"

Siobhan glanced at Elana. Elana nodded and moved up beside her. "If that happens, let the matchmaker assigned to your group know. We'll work to accommodate you."

Murmurs quieted as Pierre pushed the two-tiered cart up beside the row of tables center of the dining area. He took the lid off the first tray he placed on the table closest to him. Different raw vegetables and fresh fruit adorned the tray. Next to the tray, he set two large bowls of mixed green salad along with several bottles of salad dressing. The second tray held a variety of baked cookies and crackers with sliced cheese. Chef put the tray of burgers and buns he carried middle of the row of tables. He took the next item from Pierre, a large double-handled pot filled with steak tartare. Pierre set the second double-handled pot filled with the same next to it. The last two tables in the row held condiments, bowls of chips and pretzels.

"Those that ordered either of the specials. A buffet is set up for you at the rear of the dining area. Everyone get your food. Enjoy, mingle and non-alcoholic drinks are on the house." Chef set the tray lids on the cart, patted Pierre's shoulder and whispered. "Good luck keeping them under control. I'll be back in a moment."

Pierre laughed. "One moment before you take off with the cart. Louie, the first, needs to make his presence known." Pierre pulled the wooden bat off the second shelf of the cart, looped it in the air, and soundly laid it on the table close to him and behind the pots of steak tartare.

Chef grinned as he pushed the cart away. Siobhan had Louie number two on the shelf close to the cash register within reach, ready to grab if needed. Lance, Keith and Ty stood close to the bar, facing the dining area. Chaos wasn't going to win tonight.

Caleb moved up beside Siobhan. "Your attention, please. I am announcing my match choice. Maggie Nickerson. I am granted this privilege as Matchmakers council representative."

Several gasps sounded. Murmurs began. Caleb rapped on the table close to him. "Quiet. This is no surprise. Get your food and find someone you wish to mingle with as you eat. Siobhan will call time when it is time to begin match recordings."

Caleb turned to Siobhan. "Give them ten minutes more?"

Siobhan nodded. "No problem. They will take five to ten finding someone to sit with."

Caleb walked over to Maggie. She flipped through pages of her ledger, pointing and talking to one of her trainee assistants. "Toss a yellow, blue and pink blank slip into the hat. We'll draw one out to start with the names in that ledger section. Six at a time unless there are less, then announce how many there are."

"I'm sure you heard," Caleb said, moving closer to Maggie.

"Yeah, you declared your intent. Doesn't mean I agree." Maggie stepped away from Caleb. "I'm busy. Good luck finding someone who wants you as a match."

"I'm sure I've made the right choice. We're matched for the next thirty days. This way you can save face and let your pheromones loose. I've already caught several heady whiffs of them. I've got the hots for you too." Caleb winked and walked away.

Maggie rolled her eyes, shook her head, and glanced back at Caleb. The man gave good banter. Her thoughts went a bit further. . .was he that good with other things?

"Maggie, we're ready, right?"

Maggie jumped, glancing down at her arm. One of her assistants' hand lay on her arm. Luna above, she needed to focus on work. Not how Caleb filled out his pants. A man with junk in his trunk might have. . .how had he done it? Maggie exhaled slowly. Caleb oozed confidence. He didn't swagger, brag or boast. He spoke and carried himself with an inner confidence. She faced her assistant. "Yes, we're ready to go."

Caleb sat down in a chair close to where Ty stood. "Well, cousin, I think our parents would be proud. We've chosen strong, independent women as our matches."

Ty nodded. "I agree. Our clan's mixed leadership rules prepare any of us to lead as needed. I'm glad our parents instilled equality as a foundation in our beliefs and mores."

"Caleb," Siobhan said, approaching them. "Excuse me for interrupting. Your burger and hot chocolate are on the bar. Your dram of scotch is in the shot glass next to the mug."

"Thank you." Caleb stood. "Siobhan, I'll signal when we need to start recording matches."

Ty entwined his fingers with Siobhan's. "We ate earlier. Share a snack?"

"Yes. I have two cups of Chef's clam chowder. He said he and Pierre could share with us. Everyone gets special treatment tonight." Siobhan squeezed Ty's hand.

"Let's eat. I caught whiffs of the clam chowder every time the kitchen door swung open." Ty walked to the end of the bar close to where Caleb sat.

Siobhan sat next to Caleb. She pulled the cups of soup to her. "I hope morning sickness doesn't happen."

Caleb leaned toward her. "If it does, contact me. My aunt is a naturopath pharmacist. She can work with your doctor on natural meds. Makes life easier when you've got medical and pharmaceutical that work in tandem and get magics and shifter hybrids."

"Thanks Caleb. I appreciate the offer. Ty and I will know more in the next few days." Siobhan bit into a piece of pepper jack cheese and rye crisp cracker. She glanced at Ty as she chewed. He nodded as he tasted the clam chowder. Caleb saluted her with the shot glass, emptied part of it into his hot chocolate and stirred.

Chef stepped behind the bar and set a glass of seltzer water next to her. He squeezed two lime wedges into the water. "My mom swears by this when she eats spicy food. I have a piece of the cake Pierre made for the lunch rush ready to bring out once the music starts. Take it easy the rest of the night. Pierre, your aunt, Ty and I, along with James and Caleb have your back."

Siobhan blinked twice. This was the second time tonight she'd come close to tears. She was losing her rough edge? She blinked again. What happened to her grit, backbone, and assertive shield? She inhaled slowly, gripping her soup spoon tighter—she couldn't have what her granny called the pregnancy blues. The swing in hormones and body chemistry that caused mood swings faster than any shape shifter could shift.

"Thanks Chef. " Siobhan sipped and swallowed. Her mouth cooled as the chilled lime seltzer mixture flowed across her tongue and taste buds. Change was happening. Rate it was happening, she'd better get used to it. She set the glass down.

"Caleb, how does your sixth shifter sense read the room?" Siobhan picked up her soup cup with two hands and drank. Hints of garlic, onion and oregano tickled her taste buds. Bits of potato and clams followed. She chewed and swallowed. Her stomach gurgled and quieted. She drank more, savoring the rich broth and seasonings. She set the cup down and reached for the spoon close to her.

"There's unrest. Pheromones are flowing, hormones are pulsating, and lust is simmering. Not a great combination for tranquility. I sense a pervasive calm surrounding everyone." Caleb stirred his hot chocolate, emptied the remainder of the dram of scotch into it and stirred more. "The One and Luna are definitely present."

Siobhan nodded. "I noted a yellow aura around the edge of the room mixing with bursts of mauve and red."

"You see auras?" Caleb glanced at her.

"Yes, one of my shape shifter traits." Siobhan faced Ty. "We'll talk about this when we're alone."

Ty brushed his lips over hers. "I agree. We can do that after the tests."

Several moments passed as murmurs of conversation from the dining area reached them. Caleb continued eating. He noted where Maggie was as well as the other matchmakers. Everyone was eating. Some couples were sitting together, talking as they ate. There were a few groups of three or four sharing a table, also eating and conversing. The few loners sat at the long table quietly eating.

Some said matches couldn't be forced. Others went to a matchmaker in hopes of finding a mate. Cauldron Falls' mixture hoped for a chance for acceptance and finding someone they could be themselves with. Caleb glanced to where Maggie stood jotting names on the pad she carried. Could she be the one? The one his dreams gave him glimpses of? And the others, were they listening with their hearts and letting themselves step into the magic their hearts spun for them?

THIRTEEN

Elana moved closer to James. As they ate, she noticed the subtle changes in the room. Many sat facing each other, talking as they ate. Those who hadn't made a potential match choice sat with others who hadn't. No one was alone. Even those who sat quietly listening to the others around them smiled and nodded. Each breath she took was easier. The chaotic, hurried feeling dissipated as James slipped his arm around her shoulders and hugged her. His warmth and peace flowed off him and onto her, soaking deep into her psyche and soul. The last ninety minutes was the break she needed. Even Maggie appeared to calm down. Caleb left her alone as she ate with her trainees and assistants.

Elana kissed James's cheek and squeezed his hand. "I need to check with Zelda, Tara and Naomi."

James hugged her again. "I'm right here if you need me."

Elana rose and picked up her ledger off the table. She glanced up at the skylight as she started across the dining area. Luna's waxing and waning had started. Her light was less intense and didn't fill the skylight quite as much. There was a purpose in the magic flowing down into the area. A soft voice filled her mind. *"Do not fret. Your job here is done. You've opened hearts and minds. Your heart's joy is your joy. Be at peace."*

Elana continued counting her breaths as she exited the moon-lit area. Some said hearing Luna's and the One's message spoken directly to you was a sign. Others said pure magic happened in those moments. Connection with the cosmos and deity pulled you out of yourself and allowed you to see in new ways. Elana knew whatever happened the rest of the night, she was at peace. Perhaps her longing for the feeling of finding a home was taking place.

Elana compared Zelda's list to their ledger. Zelda's list showed twenty people matched. Tara's list showed another eight couples. Naomi's list had two groups of two couples pairing up together as quads plus an additional five couples. Elana glanced at Naomi's list again. "Naomi, why is there a circle around Franklin Moore's name?'

Naomi motioned Elana closer. "Franklin and I didn't get a chance to see if we could make a go of things in high school. He said he didn't feel drawn to any of the women with his crystal color. He asked if I'd give us another shot. Told him I'd think about it."

"Have you made up your mind?"

Naomi leaned to her left, glanced to where Franklin stood talking with Hawke and straightened. "My heart has. Franklin and I aren't getting any younger. I'm listening to my heart tonight. Franklin is getting another shot."

Elana reached for Naomi's list. "Good for you, Naomi. I hope Zelda gives Hawke another chance."

"Zelda asked Hawke when she got to him if he'd decided who his match was. He held out his crystal to her and said you, my dear. I caught a glimpse of the color of Hawke's crystal outlining them." Naomi handed her list to Elana. "I thought Kole Abernathy would be here tonight. He's talked about Tara a lot each time I've run into him."

"I'll ask Zelda in a moment." Elana glanced at her list. "No one by that name that I'm aware of. Has anyone checked Maggie's listings?"

"No. One of her assistants said they were matching colored slips of paper. Caleb hasn't let Maggie out of his sight since her assistants started collecting the slips."

A loud rap sounded. Elana and Naomi turned toward the center of the dining area. Siobhan rapped on the table close to her with Louie the first. "Dining and mingling time is over. If you haven't chosen your match yet, see the head matchmaker for each group to schedule your second chance round. Second chance rounds begin in twenty minutes. This time, you have thirty minutes to find a match of your choice or the matchmakers might choose for you."

Elana grinned. If this was like Siobhan's reports of other Sadie Hawkins Full Moon matching, no one would leave unpartnered for the next thirty days. Some great friendships and strong bonds had come from the last-moment matchups.

Tallying continued as Pierre and Chef brought out pans of sheet cakes, more cookies, and pastries. Pots of coffee and tea and assorted take-out cup sizes lined the bar. James put herbal mint tea bags and dollops of honey in two medium-sized take-out cups.

Chef held out a bag as James put lids on the cups. "Special treat from Pierre and I for you and Ms. Elana. Double peppermint chocolate brownies with a cream cheese filling."

'Thank you, Chef." James took the bag. "Elana is going to need this if we're going to stay awake much longer. "

Chef grinned. "Another ninety minutes at best. Most of the people left are sizing each other up now. Some will pair up so they won't be alone. Those usually become regular patrons on couples' nights. Let's them have time together without expectations of more."

James nodded. "Friends with benefits of the non-sexual type."

"Yup, and some of those have led to the most successful matches and romances recorded. They get to know each other without worrying about the long haul."

"Good to see that flexibility is part of matchmaking." James picked up the take-out cups. "I hope tonight's event closes out quietly."

"We'll have to see what Maggie and Caleb decide." Chef shrugged and walked away.

James made his way around the couples mingling close to the outer edge of the dining area. Maggie hadn't said much during the intermission. Caleb stood near the bar, talking with Pierre and Ty. Siobhan hadn't moved from her spot close to the outer edge of the waning moonlight coming through the open skylight. Would the evening end quietly or with more fireworks from Maggie and Caleb happening?

Elana took the cup James held out to her. "Thank you, James."

"How goes the tallying?" James broke one of the brownies in half and laid it on a napkin next to Elana's cup.

"We're at ninety-five percent. Five couples are still unsure. Zelda and Hawke are among them." Elana sipped her tea. "Naomi and Franklin are still talking."

"Maggie and Caleb?" James chuckled, pulling a chair close to Elana.

"Don't know. They're gonna have to decide soon. Keith let us know the weather report says snow is expected before dawn."

"Can we give everyone a few more moments? Check Maggie's list and see if her matches are legit?"

Elana patted James's arm. "Moments, possibly. Check for legit matches? Call people out in front of everyone? Not a good idea. Unless you want bedlam erupting."

"How about we check all matches?" Caleb squatted down next to her and James. "No offense meant to you, Zelda, Naomi or Tara. Checking all matches levels the playing field."

Elana nodded. "Caleb, you're going to have to oversee it. Non-partial observation and elvaluation."

"That I am. My job with Maggie regardless." Caleb rose. "I'll officially sanctify yours and James's match plus Siobhan and Ty's since neither of you were on any list."

James handed Caleb the last section of brownie. "Fortify yourself. Chocolate does calm some angst."

Caleb smiled.""Thanks. My stomach and sweet tooth are pacified. Now, if Maggie would. . . "

Elana held up both hands. "My turn to say TMI. Your aura runs yellow, red and back to mauve. May Luna and the One guide you personally on that."

Caleb popped his brownie bite into his mouth and walked away.

James held out his hand. "Looks like we best make our way to the front. We've got a moonlit declaration to make."

Elana clasped James's hand. Siobhan and Ty stood to Caleb's left. Maggie on his right. Her arms folded tightly across her chest, scowling. Lupa, help them all if Maggie's aura indicated what her thoughts were. Chaos and its riotous glee lurked, waiting to erupt.

Caleb rapped on the table close to him. "Everyone's attention please. As the Matchmakers' Council's representative, I am verifying all matches on each matchmaker's present list. Maggie will record them in the council's book I have with me, and Lance will witness the recording."

Murmurs and soft chatter continued. Caleb stepped into the moon lit circle. "I recognize and validate the following matches since they are not on any matchmaker's list. James and Elana, step into the circle and declare your match before all, Luna and the One."

James squeezed Elana's hand and stepped into the circle. Elana followed him into the circle, standing beside him, facing him.

"I declare Elana as my full moon match. Freely enter into this match and abide by the Sadie Hawkins full moon match for the next thirty days."

Elana clasped James's hand, holding it aloft. "I claim thee as my full moon match. Agree to abide by the Sadie Hawkins full moon match for the next thirty days. Bless Luna and the One for bringing us together." She clasped James's other hand and held it aloft next to their joined hands.

"So this match is noted, validated and verified by me as the council's representative. Please sign below Lance and Maggie's signatures." Caleb faced Siobhan and Ty. "You are next."

Siobhan and Ty repeated their full moon match declaration and signed the council's book.

"Maggie, we're next." Caleb glanced at Maggie. Would she willingly declare her agreement?

FOURTEEN

Maggie entered the circle, turned away from Caleb and faced the crowd. "I only agree to this match because the council representative decreed it. I will not cease my matchmaking business nor will I tolerate his attempts to dominate me or any of my staff or trainees. I ask Luna and the One to abide by my decision and declaration."

Gasps and whispers rippled through the crowd. Many pointed at Caleb and the Sisterhood of Three.

Caleb stepped into the circle, tilted his head back and spoke as moonlight illuminated his face. "Blessed are those that ask for your guidance, Luna and the One. I freely enter into this Sadie Hawkins full moon match for the next thirty days. I make this match outside of my council role. May Maggie and I bond together in peace, joy and a mutual understanding; love magic is random. More than names drawn out of hats or matching colored pieces of paper."

Caleb moved around Maggie until he faced her. "This match is noted, recorded and declared according to council edict and witnessed by Luna, the One and the Sisterhood of Three. We now sign the council's book."

Maggie opened her mouth, shaking her head. Caleb touched Maggie's arm. "You have spoken in front of witnesses, declared your intent within the full moon circle, and before Luna and the One." Caleb closed the space between them. He lowered his voice as he continued speaking. "Don't make an ass out of yourself going back on your word. We'll discuss us later on tonight."

"I don't think so. Nothing says I have to go with you." Maggie pulled away from him.

"No, you don't. I don't have to go with you either." Caleb lowered his hand. "Reputation matters in our line of work. When you flaunt the council's edicts and show disdain for love magic energy plus Luna and the One, you risk losing your business, your reputation and what community respect you have. Is that what you want?"

Maggie quickly shook her head no. "Let's sign the book and get on with verifying matches. We'll walk out together. After that we go our separate ways for now."

"Agreed." Caleb exited the circle, making his way to where Zelda stood holding Caleb's matchmaking council book.

Zelda stood next to Hawke. They'd quickly acknowledged their mutual interest. Touches and brushes as they reached for food ignited warm shivers up and down her arms. Hawke remembered her food allergies, offered his help when she couldn't reach something and sat on the same side of the table with her in the small booth they'd sat in. Neither had said anything about moving beyond the small talk. Zelda inhaled slowly, faced Hawke and held out the pen Caleb had handed her before he went into the circle to declare his match intention with Maggie.

"Are we ready to do it?" Zelda pointed to the book. "We don't officially have a matchmaker. It's up to us."

Hawke placed his hand on her shoulder, leaned in, pressed his lips to hers and drew back slightly. "My only question is are you sure? Ready to take that leap of trust and faith together?"

Zelda cupped Hawke's face between her hands. "Yes. I trust my heart, Luna and the One. They guided me to you tonight."

"Trusting ourselves, Luna and the One is a small part of this. Do you trust me? We've got to trust each other and talk about everything. No holding back like before." Hawke reached for the pen.

Zelda dropped her hands. "Trust is a two-way street. Do you trust me enough to go through with this?"

Hawke clasped the pen. "Yes, I do. We recognized our joint interest. Got beyond small talk as we ate. Even found out a couple of things we have in common now. I think we're ready to commit to a match. Thirty days to get reacquainted and learn more about each other's here and now."

"Caleb," Hawke called out. "Could Zelda and I talk with you a moment?"

Caleb captured Maggie's hand, pulling her with him as he turned toward Hawke and Zelda.

"Stop," Maggie yelped. "Caleb, stop. You can't drag me everywhere. I have rights. Choices and you could ask, you know. It's called manners."

"I could. You don't turn manners off and on." Caleb faced Maggie. "If I let go, are you going to sneak off? Or see what a couple needs from a matchmaker and the council's representative?"

Maggie pulled her hand away from Caleb's. "I couldn't sneak off if I wanted to. I gave my word. If this couple needs a matchmaker, I am here for them."

Caleb rubbed his knuckles across Maggie's cheek. "Thank you. Trust follows when actions and words back each other up."

"Listen to what you just said and apply it. You might be surprised what happens." Maggie stepped around him.

Caleb turned to Zelda and Hawke. "Hawke, how can Maggie and I help you?"

"Zelda and I need to declare our match choice. We're not on any matchmaker list." Hawke slipped his arm around Zelda's waist.

"I can't record and witness my own match choice." Zelda held out the council's record book. "Maggie, would you and Caleb honor us by recording and witnessing Hawke and my match choice declaration?"

Caleb nudged Maggie. Would she accept the age-old request? Or would she scoff at a matchmaker asking for help from her so-called competition?

"I'm honored to record and witness with Caleb your match choice declaration. Thank you for choosing us to be your witnesses." Maggie held out her hand to Hawke. "The pen please."

Caleb pressed his lips together. Retorts and skepticism roared loudly in his mind, ready to spew forth. He flexed his hands. Goddess and Luna, had Maggie's sarcasm bit him? As Maggie placed the book on the table closest to them and opened it, Caleb slowly exhaled. Trust required a foundation. Had Maggie just laid the first cornerstone?

"Do Zelda and I need to go into the moonlit circle?" Hawke turned toward the waning moonlit streaming in through the skylight.

"Not all match declarations require a moonlit circle. Step to the edge of the circle where Luna and the One can illuminate the book as you sign and vocally declare your Sadie Hawkins full moon match choice." Caleb pushed the table close to the edge of the circle.

Hawke and Zelda stepped into the outer edge of the circle, each partially lit by the moon.

"I, Hawke, declare my freely made match choice. Zelda, you are my full moon match choice now and beyond." Hawke raised their joined hands and kissed the back of Zelda's hand.

"Hawke, are you sure? Now and beyond?" Zelda closed the space between them until they stood toe to toe.

"Yes, I'm very sure." Hawke blew her a kiss.

"I, Zelda, declare my full moon match choice. Hawke, you are part of who I am, who I've become, and I declare I want you in my here, now and future." Zelda rubbed her cheek against their joined hands.

"I witness this match choice as the council's representative." Caleb signed next to Maggie's signature as recording matchmaker. "Please sign the book formalizing your match choice."

Maggie took the pen from Hawke as he finished signing next to Zelda's signature. "What about Tara and Naomi? Do their match choices need witnessing?"

"They're on Elana's list. They're still making their choices." Zelda slipped her arm around Hawke's waist. "Thank you, Maggie and Caleb."

Maggie watched Hawke and Zelda walk away. She watched and waited. She pressed each of her fingers against her legs, counting her breaths in and out. On the second pass of her fingers against her legs, she exhaled deeply and tipped her head back. Nothing had happened. No angst. No ire or even a tap from the green-eyed monster. Peace and contentment were the words that flashed through her thoughts. How long was this going to last? No one was complaining. People were quietly talking, and a few watched her and Caleb. Maybe—just maybe there was something to this calm and tranquility pulsating around her and rippling through her. She slowly turned. Caleb intently watched her. Let him. She'd earned these few moments of hard-won peace and contentment.

Caleb approached her, holding out his hand. "Come, I've got to verify match choices. Simple, quick and easy are my preferences. You check off the names and choices on sign-up lists vs. recorded match choice lists for Elana and the Sisterhood of Three. They will witness your actions as you cross-check the lists. They will do the same with you and your apprentices lists."

Maggie pressed her teeth tightly against her tongue. Sarcastic retorts and comeback bubbled and frothed, ready to spill out. Defending herself was so second nature. She glanced up at the moon still slightly over head, its light touching part of her face.

Maggie closed her eyes and sent forth her heartfelt prayer. *Luna and the One, please hear my prayer. I want this moment of peace and contentment to last. To continue even as you move across the sky, making way for morning light. I don't want to fear and cower, waiting to defend myself. Thank you.*

She opened her eyes. Caleb stood in front of her, his hands at his sides. He nodded. Had he heard her prayer? Could he read her mind?

"Your communication with Luna and the One is safe." Caleb pointed at the skylight. "Let's get on with the verifications. Frosted panes aren't good."

Siobhan rapped on the bar. "Attention please. Verifications are going to need to happen rapidly. Snow is falling. Temperature is dropping. We're closing early to ensure all get home safely."

Caleb called out, standing on a chair close to the front of the group. "Lists and matchmakers to the bar. Zelda and Hawke will verify Maggie's list. Maggie and I will verify Elana's list. James and Siobhan will verify the Sisterhood's list. Any unmatched people choose now so Lance and Keith can record them."

Thirty minutes passed while each couple listed confirmed their match choice and thirty-day commitment. The remaining four couples declared their interest in matching up as a quad. Caleb stuffed the lists into the council book and placed it in his backpack. He rapped on the bar. "All matches are verified. Safe journey home, everyone. This Sadie Hawkins full moon match event is finished, closed, and recorded."

FIFTEEN

Couples scrambled into their coats and jackets. Many made their way out the door, grabbing bags of food off the bar. Chef and Pierre filled the empty spots with a few more bags.

Caleb wrapped his neck scarf around his neck, buttoned up his coat and faced Maggie. "My place is out beyond the edge of town. The roads may be too dicey to make it home. In-town hotels are full. Looks like you got company for the next few days."

"Days?" Maggie zipped up her jacket. "What makes you think that's happening?"

Lance walked by them, brushing the snow off his jacket. "Weather report is hard freeze overnight and twelve inches plus snowfall."

"Are you prepared to stay somewhere other than your place?" Caleb slipped his backpack over one shoulder. "Seriously, you got someone here you can stay with? Can you make it home?"

Maggie put her purse in her tote bag and set it on the bar. "All-wheel drive car. Snow tires and full tank of gas. Five miles to my place. Maybe twenty to twenty-minute drive in this weather."

"Good. I'll get my duffle bag out of my car." Caleb started toward the door. "Grab a couple bags of leftovers. I'll meet you at your car."

Maggie glanced at Elana, James, Siobhan and Ty. "I told him no."

Elana put the last two bags of leftovers in Maggie's tote bag. "Maggie, best piece of advice any of us can give you is go with the flow. Nothing says you have to sleep with him. You do have a guest room, right?"

Maggie grinned, picked up her tote bag and started toward the exit. She turned around. "Elana, why are you giving me advice?"

"Suggestion. Just a suggestion." Elana stepped closer. "Maggie, sometimes the person who isn't in the middle of things sees it differently. You and Caleb can either partner on this thirty-day adventure or be at odds. Stepping back, evening the playing field and talking might work."

Maggie nodded. "Thanks. Caleb and I have a lot to talk about and work out."

Elana smiled. "One last thing. Know when to yield and when to stand your ground. Think before you speak. Listen to your heart and psyche. Luna and the One will guide you."

Maggie reached for the door as Caleb and a blast of arctic wind shoved the door open. Caleb faced her, holding his duffle bag. His wind-swept hair looked like he'd jumped out of bed, tossed on his clothes and raced out the door. This unreserved look...she wasn't going to let her thoughts wander. Getting her and her company home safely was a priority. Her psyche could shut up. Sleeping alone in a kingsize bed wasn't an issue. Nor was the male that pinged her in several places sharing it. His choices were the guest room or the couch.

"You ready?" Caleb moved toward her.

"I am ready to go home." Maggie sidestepped Caleb, pulled the door open and continued speaking. "You can decide if you want the guest room or the couch once I get us there."

Caleb glanced at Siobhan. She shrugged. James and Ty shrugged too. Elana pointed toward the rapidly closing door. "Best hurry along. You might miss your ride."

Caleb rushed out the door, calling for Maggie to wait up.

Siobhan faced Elana, a huge cheshire cat-like grin starting. "I think those two have met their match. And I'm not referring to their full moon one."

Ty chortled. "We probably should check in with them later to make sure they got to Maggie's okay."

"Might be doable if we had either of their cell phone numbers." James buttoned his coat and turned up the collar.

Elana held out her knitted hat to James. "You're going to need this. That wind blast Caleb let in was bitter. I'll use my scarf to cover my head and neck."

Siobhan faced Ty. "You're coming with us. Easier to get to my place than you trying to drive through town and navigate the incline to your place's parking lot."

"Agreed." Ty zipped up his jacket and put his earmuffs on. "Everything locked up? Pierre and Chef ready to leave too?"

"We sure are," Pierre called out, exiting the kitchen. "Chef locked the cash drawer in the safe along with the day's receipts and deposit."

"All right," Chef said, moving up beside the group. "We're staying with my Aunt Stella and her husband Ethan. She lives one building over from yours, Siobhan. We'll follow you there."

Ten minutes later, the last two vehicles pulled out of Sadie's parking lot. How each of their rides home would go, none of them knew.

Halfway down Pine Ridge Road, Maggie glanced at Caleb. He hadn't said a word since she told him to fasten his seatbelt, keep his driving tips to himself, and as her co-pilot, he could keep an eye on the road for ice and watch the signs for Star Gaze Lane. The tension simmering between them was thick enough to boil over. Watching Caleb out of the corner of her eye each time she stopped at a traffic light or stop sign, she caught bits and pieces of his aura. Blues, hazels and reds mixed with tinges of yellow. Aura magic and reading wasn't one of her strong magics. If she remembered her aura reading class training, Caleb was turned on, a bit frightened and a whole lot trying to shield. Why? She didn't have time to ask. Snow was falling faster and blowing as the wind picked up.

"How much farther down this unlit road do we need to go?" Caleb shifted in his seat, reaching up and gripping the passenger side grab handle.

"About a mile unless we use Ford Creek Bridge. It's probably iced over." Maggie eased to the side of the road. "You can let go of the grab bar. I'm not jeopardizing our lives."

Caleb turned in his seat, facing her. "Sorry. I'm used to doing the driving in snow storms. I don't handle being a passenger well."

"Understood. I don't like driving in snow storms. Had to learn how since I was on my own." Maggie put the car into gear. "I say we ease on down the road. Let Ford Creek Bridge be for tonight."

Caleb nodded. "Can I ask you something?"

"Nothing distracting." Maggie maneuvered the car back into the tire tracks she could make out thanks to the car's high beam lights.

"Do you hate me?"

Maggie gripped the steering wheel harder. She said nothing distracting. The question was a simple yes or no. Straightforward inquiry for sure.

"Hate is too strong." She slowed as they came to an intersection. "What does that sign say?"

"Claremont Passing Court." Caleb let go of the grabbar. "I think the partially snow-covered sign said Star Gaze Lane next turn."

"Thanks." Maggie crept through the intersection and put on her turn signal. "Star Gaze Lane isn't well marked. County put up that sign to let folks know they were approaching. New development hasn't gotten okay for signage and lighting yet."

"Is that dark spot the intersection?" Caleb tapped on the windshield.

"Sure is. Thanks for spotting it." Maggie made a wide turn, placing them in the middle of the intersection.

"What if another car comes toward us?" Caleb grabbed the grab handle again.

Maggie laughed. "In this weather, not even a goose flying ass backwards blind with a fog light and air horn would be tempting fate."

"A what?" Caleb wrapped his other hand around the grab handle, tightly gripping it.

"Never mind, we're going in." Maggie gunned the motor. Tires spun, kicking snow and ice into the air. The car jumped forward.

Caleb started muttering in a low, bearly audible voice.

"I don't know if you're praying or cussing." Maggie chortled. "That's the gravel patch the county and city are fighting over who's responsible for paving the last three feet of road."

"They can add repadding my ass to the list!" Caleb let a few more cuss words fly.

"I don't think those words have much magic value." Maggie slowed the car as the apron of the parking entrance appeared. Two large golden dots appeared at the outer edge of the partially lit lot.

"What in the name of Luna, is that?" Caleb tapped the windshield and pointed.

"Luther, the parking lot gargoyle." Maggie headed toward the glowing dots that got closer and brighter.

"Parking lot gargoyle?" Caleb slowly inhaled. Who's magic was addled and very off-kilter?

"Yes, he's quite a nice gargoyle. Takes three hundred-watt light bulbs for each of his eyes. Mack will change them out for flashing red, green and silver ones in a couple of days." Maggie slowed the closer they got to Luther. She slowly turned the car as four houses came into view. "Wait until you see Sheila. We got her solstice ready, and she's looking fine."

Caleb exhaled, glanced at Maggie and let go of the grab handle. "These gargoyles are inanimate, yes?"

"Depends on your view. Most of the kids in the complex community talk to them daily." Maggie stopped in front of a small single-story house. "Me, I just thank each of them for guarding the parking lot and our cars."

Caleb unfastened his seatbelt. Either Maggie was bsing him or the dram of scotch he drank hit him harder than he thought it had. He'd met a few dragon shifters that bore keeping an eye on. Had a few immigrated from Europe to Cauldron Falls?

SIXTEEN

Ty leaned toward Siobhan as she started the car. "Keith ran out to the corner pharmacy earlier. He's holing up at his girlfriend's place. He picked up our order along with his."

Siobhan nodded. She glanced in the rearview mirror. James and Elana were cuddled against each other, holding hands and talking quietly. They looked up, smiled, and nodded. Could she and Ty find similar tranquility? Would they bicker like her parents did? Often agreeing to disagree on how to raise their children? She didn't want that kind of relationship. She wanted—and needed—peace, quiet and, if she and Ty argued for it not to turn into shouting matches that sent their child running, hiding and crying. Luna and the One help them both to embrace supporting each other and not have their child running to hide under the bed, scared to come out, and crying every time someone raised their voice.

"I'll thank Keith next time I see him." Siobhan refocused on the road. Snow fell faster than when they left Sadie's ten minutes ago. Tire tracks from other cars quickly filled as the flakes came down. "Are Chef and Pierre behind us?"

Ty glanced in the side mirror. "There's another vehicle two car lengths behind us. I think it's them."

"Chef wrote their license plate down for me and I did the same with yours Siobhan. James swiped his gloved hand across the rear window. "I can make out part of the license plate. It's them."

"Good." Siobhan gripped the wheel tighter. "Patches of bare road are probably icy. Black ice. Worst kind."

"Are we going to be able to get into the parking lot?" Ty laid his hand on her arm. "I'd offer to drive, but it's too late for that."

Siobhan snickered. "Yeah, cuz me and black ice have a love-hate relationship. It loves to find me and bruise my ass. I hate dealing with it any more than I have to."

"None of us wants to wrestle with black ice tonight. I'm fine with Siobhan driving." Elana chimed in. "After all, I taught her how to drive."

"Yup, my parents were to busy arguing about who should."

"I'm glad Elana and I were part of your youth Siobhan." James leaned forward and patted her shoulder. "I think we best let her concentrate on her driving."

"Thanks James. I'm glad you and Aunt Elana are part of my chosen and blood family." Siobhan tapped on the brake pedal and put on the right blinker. "Okay we're going in. Everyone hold on. The apron's crusted with snow and ice."

The car inched up the apron incline. It's tire spinning and spraying ice and snow. Siobhan pressed the gas pedal slowly, turning the steering wheel to the right. The car shot forward, clearing two patches of ice, landing with a loud thud.

"Wow!" James clasped his seatbelt shoulder strap tightly between his hands. "Nice maneuver. Could we skip the flight for the rest of the trip?"

Elana slowly exhaled. "I agree with James. Siobhan, how much further till we're in the lot and able to park?"

Ty tapped on the windshield. "Siobhan, high beams, please. I think we're almost in."

Siobhan turned on the high beams, illuminating several open parking spaces in front of them. Patches of plowed pavement showed at the outer edges of the headlight beam. "Ty, open your window and tell what you see toward the back wheel."

"I'll check my side," James said, opening his window. "Look like we're caddy cornered on the apron."

"Are the rear wheels over the ice hump, James?" Siobhan glanced at Ty. "Ty, front wheels?"

"How about we all check and decide what's next?" Elana opened her window, leaning partially out. "This side is just clear of the ice hump."

"Same on my side," James added, closing his window. "Wind is kicking up again."

"Ty?" Siobhan asked, opening her window.

"Front wheel on passenger side is almost on clear pavement." Ty closed his window.

Siobhan put the car in park, gripped the steering wheel with both hands as she leaned out the driver's side window. Bits of ice pelted her cheeks, stinging with each wind blast pelting the car. She squinted, slowly looked forward toward where the headlight beam began and back to the dimly lit shadow of the front tire. Clear pavement ahead. If she backed up, ice hump wrestling round two. Forward jerky moves might be their best option.

"Hold on." Siobhan closed her window. "We're going in. An inch at a time if necessary."

She put the car into gear and tapped on the gas pedal. The car jerked, tires spinning, and jumped forward. Ice and snow filled the rearview mirror's view. Siobhan turned the steering wheel to the right, hoping the clear pavement didn't include black ice. No cars came into view. The outdoor lights of her building slowly came into view as the car crept forward. Two feet driving was her best option. Right foot on the gas pedal, accelerating as needed. Her left on the brake. She hadn't driven like that since she almost stripped the gears of her uncle's car's manual transmission trying to learn how to drive a stick shift.

Elana patted her shoulder. "I'm sure Uncle Auggie is shrieking and cussing in his ethereal form."

Siobhan nodded. "That and plenty of his hand gestures."

"That's why I took over teaching you how to drive." Elana glanced at James. "With James's help, we got you over your fear of getting behind the wheel and driving."

"Sure did." James chuckled. "Auggie wasn't cut out to teach more than cussing, fussing and gesturing as a fast take course."

"There's two parking spaces in front of your building." Ty tapped the windshield. "Are Chef and Pierre still behind us?"

"As Uncle Auggie used to say, 'Them blasted lights behind us ain't spooks,'" Siobhan quipped in her best deep voice.

Laughter filled the car as Siobhan parked the car in one of the empty parking spaces. Chef and Pierre pulled in beside them. Everyone arrived safe and sound. The front walkway looked safe to cross. Chef got out first, slowly making his way around his car. His hands never moved far from the hood.

Pierre opened his door and cautiously stepped out. He tapped on Siobhan's window. "Doesn't appear slippery. Let's get in the lobby with what we can carry. Chef, Ty and I can come back for the rest."

Ty slipped his backpack on and reached for Siobhan's duffle.

"I can take that." Siobhan clutched the duffle's handles. "I'm not helpless."

"None of us are," Elana said, opening the driver's side back door. "If we help each other, we get in quicker and safer."

"Elana's got her bag." James got out and closed the passenger-side back door. "I can carry something."

Pierre faced Chef as he came around the hood of the car. "Anything besides our packs and the two bags of food?"

"None. Everything is on your side in the back seat." Chef held his hand out to Siobhan. "Sidewalk is fairly clear. Some deicer crystals in places. If you take your time and get on to the grass, not much to worry about."

"Thank you Chef. I can take a food bag." Siobhan let go of her duffle, clasped Chef's hand and exited her car. "Which building is your aunt's?"

"The one next to yours." Chef helped Siobhan up onto the sidewalk. "We can take the interior connecting hallway on the first floor through the parking garage to get there."

Pierre stepped up beside them. He handed Chef his backpack. "Siobhan, Ty's got your duffle. Here's a bag of food for you."

"Thanks, Pierre." Siobhan started back toward the car. "I told Ty I could take my duffle."

"Let Ty handle it." Chef moved closer to Siobhan. "Not worth arguing about. Sooner we get inside, the better off we all are."

Siobhan pressed her lips tightly together. Letting others help her was a rough patch for her. She'd been on her own more than she could remember having people around she could count on. Accepting help didn't signal weakness. Folks came to matchmakers for help. Some to legitimize their choices. Some due to customs and folkways. Tonight, she was accepting help from everyone, even herself. Keeping the peace and working as a team took priority.

"Everybody got what they need?" Siobhan held up her bag.

Five yeses followed as each held up what they carried.

Ty stepped up on the sidewalk and turned, holding out his hand to Elana.

"Thank you, Ty." Elana grasped his hand and made her way carefully across the walk onto the grass.

"Pierre, I'll take your bag. You help James." Chef took both bags and moved onto the grass as Pierre helped James onto the walk.

Moments of cautious stepping and looking passed with Ty leading the way. Pierre and Chef brought up the rear. All wiped their feet, high-fiving each other as they entered the lobby.

"I'm glad that's over." Chef pushed the button for the elevator. "Getting to our aunt's place will be easy compared to this."

"Thank you for helping out." Siobhan pressed the door open button on the inside panel of the elevator going up. Elana, James and Ty entered, waving as the door closed.

"Aunt Stella and Ethan are still up waiting for us." Chef and Pierre entered the second elevator. "Hard to believe they're celebrating their first anniversary in a few days."

SEVENTEEN

Siobhan locked her condo door and turned. Ty, Elana and James stood next to the couch, watching her intently. When had the elephant herd appeared? The quizzical look on each of their faces made her shudder.

Ty wanted the pregnancy test done tonight. James kept squeezing her hand in the elevator like he was her balancing fulcrum. Elana had patted her arm twice. Could any of them understand her desire to sleep? To forget about what might be and luxuriate in dreams that let her relax and rest?

Siobhan set the food bag she carried on the table next to the couch and took off her jacket. She tossed it on the back of the couch. "Can you all sit down for a moment?"

Ty tossed his jacket close to hers on the back of the couch and sat down. James laid his and Elana's coats on the arm of the couch. He sat down in the wingback armchair across from it. Elana sat on the couch.

Siobhan perched on the arm of the couch as she spoke. "We got here. We're safe. The storm is peaking. It's been a long day and eventful night. I think we all need downtime."

"Agreed." Elana started to rise.

"A couple more things Aunt Elana, please." Siobhan stood. "Ty, pregnancy test can wait until tomorrow. I need sleep. So do you."

Ty yawned and nodded. "Sure. That's fine."

Siobhan faced James. "I'm okay. Thanks for helping out tonight."

James smiled. "You're welcome. I want to help any way I can."

Siobhan picked up the food bag. "I've got the munchies. How about a quick snack and we turn in?"

"I saw some chamomile tea bags in the cupboard earlier." Elana started toward the kitchen. "How about a mug for each of us?"

"I'll help," James said, following Elana into the kitchen.

"If I am pregnant, peace and rest are top priorities." Siobhan faced Ty as he stood. "One of my neighbors is a nurse practitioner. She gave me a list of dos and don'ts plus several pamphlets and a book to read."

"Good." Ty hastily hugged her and let go. "We'll go over them together. You, me, Aunt Elana and James."

"If James and Aunt Elana want to be included." Siobhan yawned. "Let's put the food up, get a snack and go to sleep."

Ty followed Siobhan into the kitchen. He hoped Maggie and Caleb, plus all the others from the Sadie Hawkins event, made it home safely.

Maggie glanced at Caleb, waiting for the garage door to finish opening. Caleb still held on to the grab bar, facing forward. They'd hit one patch of ice entering the cul-du-sac. They'd spun around for a moment. Guess Caleb didn't find a spinning car funny.

"You can let go." Maggie turned the ignition off. "We're in the garage."

Caleb slowly lowered his arm. "Yeah, I can see that."

"Then why are you turning green?" Maggie grabbed the plastic bag she kept in the center console, holding it out to Caleb.

"I'm not turning." Caleb grabbed the bag. "I'm green already!"

Coughing and barfing sounded for a few moments. Caleb wiped his mouth with the napkin Maggie tossed in his lap. He put the napkin in the plastic bag and tied it shut.

"Hope your trash can is close by." Caleb opened the passenger door.

"Over in the corner." Maggie touched his arm. "Are you coming down with something?"

"Don't think so." Caleb exited the car. "Between bolting my dinner down, a bit too much whiskey and sweets, plus. . ." He didn't say more.

Maggie reached into the back seat, grabbing her tote bag and one of the two food bags out of the back seat. She closed the driver's door and entered the code to disarm the house security system. She turned toward Caleb, who leaned against the car. "Vertigo got ya?"

Caleb looked up. He shot her a weak grin. "Happens from time to time. We all got our weaknesses to deal with. I usually keep mine well hid."

Maggie rolled her eyes, not hiding her dismay. "Letting your mortal out as my granny used to say. Nothing wrong with that."

Caleb shrugged. "Let me get my stuff. Do you have anything else to bring in?"

"Food bag on your side. Do you need help?" Maggie turned back to the door, unlocking it.

"No. Thanks for the help offer."

Maggie bounded up the steps into the house. Lemon ginger tea and scones would help settle Caleb's stomach. He'd shared a bit more of his inner self in the last few moments. Snatches of his personal side leaked out as he was undoubtedly going to say when she commented on the ride home. She'd let a few of hers out too. Would she admit fear threatened to grab control as the car damn near spun out? Not now. Not tonight. They needed sleep. They'd made it this far. Weathered a few scary patches. Blasted ice storm passed. Rapidly falling snow would accumulate overnight. Hopefully, the temperature wouldn't drop more. The outside thermometer showed twenty-five degrees as they pulled into the garage.

"You're welcome." Maggie turned on the interior lights, calling back over her shoulder. "Welcome to my abode."

Caleb clenched the straps of his duffle in one hand and the food bag in his other. His stomach flipflopped a couple of times as he gazed at the open door where Maggie stood watching him. Lupa, they'd made it here in one piece. His conscience kept replaying the hellish ride his cousin put him through learning to drive in the snow down an ice-covered road part way up the mountain to the ski resort the cousin's family owned and farmed. Nasty curves and sheer drop-offs that gave him nightmares for months.

He could stand still, caught up in past memories or move forward and make new ones. The past couldn't change. The future's foundation started now with what he did next. One step ahead and banishing the nightmares commenced. Caleb inhaled, moved around the front of Maggie's car and up the steps. He didn't pause at the entryway nor look back. Forward was where he needed to go. On into safety and a mixture of knowns and unknowns. He and Maggie were going to find out a lot about each other over the next few days.

Caleb glanced behind him as he stepped over the threshold into Maggie's home. No ghosts waited to haunt him. A thin beam of light pierced through the cloud cover and falling snow. Moonlight touched the top step and vanished. Had Luna and the One signaled he made a good decision?

Acknowledging his decision to move into the future with more unknowns than knowns? Moment by moment, he and Maggie would find out together.

Maggie pushed the button to close the garage door. She latched and secured the interior door as Caleb moved past her. "Watch out for Midnight."

Caleb glanced at his watch. "We've got a half hour to go."

"Not that Midnight. My familiars, Midnight and Nocturne." Maggie opened the refrigerator and set both food bags inside. "I hope you aren't allergic to cats."

"Cats?" Caleb set his duffle on the floor close to his feet. "Familiars?"

As if on cue, two yowls sounded. Two sets of golden yellow eyes peered out at them from on top of the refrigerator. Thuds followed as two medium-sized black cats leapt onto the floor, yowling and rubbing up against Maggie's legs.

"Yes, cat familiars." Maggie got two dishes from the dish drainer on the counter. "A lot of modern witches and supernaturals don't have animal familiars. Shape shifters' animal halves are their familiars, is my understanding."

She filled the dishes with a mixture of kibble and wet food and set them on the floor close to what he assumed was a pet water fountain. He watched while she petted the cats, murmuring softly to them as they ate. Maggie had a softer side to her?

Maggie stood. "You want some Lemon Ginger Tea and a scone?"

"Tea, yeah." Caleb picked up his duffle. "Not sure about the scone."

Maggie pointed at his duffle. "You make up your mind where you gonna sleep?"

Caleb stepped toward Maggie. "Why not with you? A lot warmer with two bodies and shared blankets. A lot less lonely too."

"Didn't offer you with me, remember?" Maggie filled the tea kettle and plugged it in. "Look, I'm not interested in arguing about shared space privileges. Get it straight here and now. My bed isn't one of those at the moment. Maybe your entire stay."

Caleb shrugged. "What if the electric goes out? How do we keep warm then?"

"Extra blankets. It's not like the entire house is going to be a deep freeze." Maggie tossed two lemon ginger tea bags into the mugs. She placed the honey container next to them. "Besides the cats sleep with me."

"You got spare heaters and don't want to share." Caleb sighed. "Not nice to deprive your guest of the added warmth."

"Cats sleep where they want. Sometimes the guest room bed." Maggie unplugged the tea kettle as it started to whistle. She filled the mugs and dumped the remaining water out. She faced Caleb. "You got one chance to have shared warmth dude! Sleeping bag on top of the covers on my bed or sleeping bag under them and you zipped up in it. Your choice. Tea's ready."

Caleb sat in the chair closest to him. Maggie set the mugs on the table. Next to them, she placed spoons and the honey pot middle of the table. She placed a plate with two scones on it next to the honey pot. Maggie sat across from him, not looking at him as she honeyed and stirred her tea. He reached for the spoon near him. If he chose the sleeping bag, he hoped it wasn't a mummy one. Getting out of it was damn near impossible if he needed to use the bathroom in the middle of the night. Though imagining Maggie's consternation when he asked for help might be worth it. He'd have to think on that aspect a bit more. He pressed his lips together, hoping his grin didn't show.

EIGHTEEN

Maggie bit into the scone she'd warmed in the microwave. Subtle hints of cinnamon and nutmeg flowed over her tastebuds as she chewed. She swallowed, sipped some of her tea and looked up. Caleb was petting Nocturne as she sat close to him. Nothing to change her opinion so far. Nocturne let most people pet her and scratch her chin. Midnight perched on the counter not far from the table. Her tail twitched each time Caleb looked her way.

Caleb picked up his mug, saluted Maggie with it, and sipped. "What flavor is the scone?"

"Cinnamon and nutmeg. Kole Abernathy bought Maddoxx's restaurant and the bakery next door. One of Ryan Butler's staff took over as head baker at the bakery. Kole dropped the day-old scones off at the floral shop Tara from the Sisterhood of Three owns." Maggie dunked the last of her scone in her tea and ate it.

Caleb tore his scone in half, held the half close to his nose and sniffed. Saigon cinnamon laced with nutmeg teased his nostrils. Flashes of his great-grandmother's homemade cinnamon candy raced through his mind. Hours spent helping her mix and make the candy were high points of his early childhood holiday memories. Another signal from Luna and the One that Maggie might be the one he saw in his dreams?

He took a bite, savoring the cinnamon sharpness followed by the nutmeg. He sipped his tea, enjoying the tartness of the lemon and ginger with the cinnamon. His mouth and tongue warmed as he continued to eat and drink. As he drank the last of his tea, he noticed how relaxed he felt. His stomach pangs were gone. He blinked and yawned. The clock above the kitchen sink showed a little after midnight. He hoped Maggie wasn't going to argue about sleeping arrangements more. Caleb put his spoon in his mug and picked it up along with the empty plate. He placed them in the sink. He faced Maggie. "I'm willing to do the sleeping bag if it isn't a mummy one. I'd sleep better knowing we were both safe and warm."

Maggie put her mug and spoon in the sink. She ran water in both mugs. As she dried her hands, she spoke. "The storm has picked up. It's probably better we're in the same room. Come on, let's get upstairs."

Caleb grabbed his duffle and followed Maggie out of the kitchen. She still hadn't answered him on the sleeping bag. Luna help him that she didn't have a mummy one. "You haven't answered me about the sleeping bag."

"Nothing says I have to." Maggie spun around and faced him. "You gonna have to wait and see."

Caleb swallowed hard. Why did Maggie's aura show she was the one? The one who's aura he kept seeing in his dreams. Deities help him. Had he gotten in over his head? He could hear the laughter and gossip after he reported to the council his observations. Thank Luna, he didn't have to include his personal ones.

"No, you don't have to say." Caleb closed the distance between him and Maggie. "I'm going to need your help getting out of the mummy bag if nature calls in the middle of the night."

Maggie chortled. "It's after midnight already. I would think you would want to know where the bathroom is in case the lights go out. Maybe even have a flashlight handy."

Damn she had him there. He did need to use the bathroom soon. If his stomach started flip-flopping again, he'd definitely need to know where the bathroom was. A flashlight would help immensely with finding his way if the lights kept flickering.

"Okay, we can keep on bantering, trying to outdo each other or one of us can. . ." How did he say yield without sounding like he was being manipulative? If he said he yielded, Maggie would scoff and probably tell him she didn't believe him much. Was there a way out of this stalemate?

Maggie yawned. "We can keep trying to outdo each other or we can call a truce."

Caleb nodded. "A truce sounds wonderful. Sleep and the bathroom are priorities, please."

Maggie thrust out her hand. "Shake on it."

Caleb pressed his lips together, hoping he thwarted the retort his tired mind and ego readily brewed. He swiped his hand on his jeans and extended his hand. "Sure. Shake and agree we work on keeping each other safe and warm without further verbal sparring."

Maggie glanced at his hand and up at him. "I agree." She firmly gripped his hand and shook it.

Heat crossed his palm, searing deep into him. White, followed by red sparks and yellow bursts, outlined their joined hands.

Maggie tried to pull her hand away. "Let go. Why is your hand so hot?"

"Aura sparks," Caleb tried to pull his hand away. "Full moon love magic and aura sparks. We got zapped by both."

"I don't love you." Maggie grabbed her wrist with her other hand and pulled her hand toward her. "Tolerating you is about as good as it gets, dude!"

Caleb inhaled, pressing his lips together. Laughter, deep belly laughter, pushed upwards, pressing to escape. Maggie didn't know that love magic didn't read your conscious mind. It swept down into the air, penetrating the hearts and psyche of the unmatched present. It, along with Luna's illuminating aura, sparks read who was the one for each present. The council swore that the old-time law was matchmakers stayed single until they no longer could make matches. Upon the translation of an ancient tome predating the first reveal during the first Celtic era.

"Why you grinning like a Cheshire cat?" Maggie rubbed her wrist, trying to work her fingers between her and Caleb's palms.

"The two of us." Caleb snickered and snorted. "We keep fighting against the magic we are part of. The sooner we accept we're together, the sooner we get to bed and sleep."

"Okay. Okay." Maggie let go of her wrist and held up her free hand. "For tonight, I yield to Luna and the One. Caleb and I are together. Can we please now get some sleep?"

Her palm chilled. Lightning flashed, and thunder rattled the windows. Caleb extracted his palm from hers. Maggie turned her hand over twice, checking the top and palm of her hand. No burn marks. No red streaks.

"My bedroom is at the end of the hall. Bathroom next to it. This first room is the guest room. The smaller room is my office." Maggie continued down the hall using the flashlight on her phone to light the way.

"There aren't lights back here?" Caleb asked, following close behind her.

"There are. I'm not chancing them going out on us." Maggie stopped next to the last door in the hall, illuminated by part of her flashlight beam. "Here's the deal. The sleeping bag zipper is broke. You need to get the pillows from the guest room cuz we're building a bundling boundary."

"A what?"

"Bundling boundary that goes down the middle of the bed." Maggie entered her bedroom. "Come on and get one of the spare flashlights. The sooner we get the boundary built, the sooner we get in bed."

Caleb shook his head, grateful Maggie couldn't see his response. Extra pillows, sleeping bag cover. Was he going to get to brush his teeth? Empty his bladder?

"I'll get the pillows after I use the bathroom." Caleb set his duffle on the floor next to the kingsize bed.

Maggie rummaged in the nightstand drawer closest to her. She clicked on the flashlight she held out. "Sure. We can figure out who gets what side after that."

Caleb nodded, doubting Maggie could see his response. He turned, ready to exit the bedroom. Two sets of golden eyes watched him from the hallway. Last cat he slept with was his grandmother's Persian, who insisted on sleeping close to his head and flapping her tail across his nose until he sneezed. His grandmother didn't get that Nataha and his love-hate relationship was more dislike-driven than any real tolerance of each other. "I think your cats have a say on the sides, too."

He stepped into the dark hall, pointing the light opposite the way they'd come. Two open doors caught part of the flashlight's beam as he swept it across the dark area in front of him. One was the bathroom for sure. He stepped forward, counting each step, knowing making his way back to the bedroom might include knowing that. As he got closer to the open doorway nearest to him, he could make out the white porcelain pedestal sink and commode. He pushed the door to, laid the flashlight on the back of the toilet, and thankful he'd guessed right. A few moments later, he washed and dried his hands, noting the running water sound indicated no frozen pipes to deal with. Had the other patrons and matchmakers made it to home or shelter?

NINETEEN

Siobhan yawned and huddled deeper into her pillows and blankets. Ty snored softly next to her. Aunt Elana and James had turned in at the same time the lights flickered, and darkness enveloped the condo. They'd turned on their cell phone flashlight function as if on queue. Fumbling in the dark in the bathroom reminded her of campouts and trying to find the tent zipper to get out to use the outhouse. She smiled, ready to go back to sleep.

Ty opened one eye, blinked and yawned. "Morning, I think."

Siobhan snuggled closer to him. "Could be."

Ty chuckled, closing the space between them until no space remained between them. "Light enough in here for the sun to be up."

"Yup." Siobhan cupped his cheek. "First decent night's sleep I've had in weeks."

"You need to close the bar earlier." Ty pulled the blanket and sheet higher, covering their arms and shoulders.

"Easier said than done." Siobhan stretched beneath the covers. "Solstice two days away. Sadie Hawkins full moon last night. Business booming."

"What if you're pregnant?" Ty slid his hand down until it rested on Siobhan's stomach. "You've gotta take care of you and the baby."

Siobhan slowly exhaled, gazing at him intently. Ty knew that look. She weighed her response. Either she was going to blast him or he'd struck a nerve. He pressed his lips together, ready to stifle his retort. This wasn't a him or her moment. It was them together, facing a future they'd either build together or destroy before it formed.

"Part of me rebells at being told what to do." Siobhan laid her hand on his, on her stomach. "You're right if I am pregnant. I need caring as much as the little one inside me."

"Not easy accepting we need help." Ty pressed his lips against Siobhan's and pulled back. "New territory for both of us. Take the pregnancy test when you're ready."

"It's today. Just later." Siobhan rolled on her other side. "I need more sleep."

Ty slipped his arm around Siobhan as he cuddled closer to her. "More sleep it is."

Their eyes closed as their breathing deepened and sleep once again claimed them.

Elana stood, stretched and moved around the foot of the bed, heading to the bathroom. James rolled over and continued snoring. Elana smiled. Last night in their haste to get into bed, neither of them had done more than strip and pull on the sweatshirts James had pulled out of the bottom drawer where Siobhan had said they were. Each sweatshirt bore a slogan. The front of James's read 'Best Place to get. . .' and the back read 'Matched at Sadie's'. Hers read 'Free Matches. Apply Within' with Sadie's logo on the back. Probably free advertising gimmicks that hadn't panned out. couns sweatshirt had barely covered his groin. His erection had bumped and rubbed against her as they quickly cuddled and settled in for sleep. Her sweatshirt came down to her mid-thighs. She had no complaints about where the sweatshirts covered and didn't. Fondles and caresses were easy when the areas that needed them were within uncomplicated reach.

She shielded her eyes as she entered the bathroom. Daylight streamed through the partially closed blind covering the small window. As Elana washed and dried her hands, she glanced out the window. Frost and ice decorated parts of the window. Snow clung to the corners. Icy flakes scattered across the frost and ice, briefly clinging and disappearing as the wind kicked up and died down. Any plans for venturing out rapidly faded.

"Warmer in there than out here cuddling with me?"

Elana smirked as she turned back toward the door. Scolding her, was he? Sarcastic crack? James's tone belied his smart-ass tone. He sounded more half asleep and trying to wisecrack. She stepped to the door and peered around the frame. "Your cock is a great place to warm up my cold hands."

"Trying to dowse the fun before it begins?" James clutched the covers, shaking his head. He grinned and winked.

"Not really." Elana quickened her pace around the bed, grabbed the covers and fanned them twice, then got in, draping the blanket and sheet partly over her. "Don't want Siobhan and Ty walking on us either."

James moved closer to her. "They're probably busy keeping warm too. Possibly the same way."

Elana turned on her side, facing James. "Could be. Doubt it."

"Oh?"

"Daylight. Bright and cold if the bathroom window is any indication of outside temp."

James yawned and stretched. "You wanna get up instead of. . ."

"Didn't say that." Elana slid her hand under the covers, slowly inching it down James's chest. "Not into quickies anymore. You?"

"No quickies." James laid his hand on hers. "Warm hands on both our parts make igniting things much easier and fulfilling."

'So true. So true." Elana pressed her lips to James's. She pulled back a bit, awaiting his reaction. James puckered his lips and ignited the kiss full throttle.

Their lips parted. Tongues touched, dueled and touched again. Mint mixed with each of their unique tastes flowed across their tastebuds, pulling them deeper into the pool of mutual passion they created.

James slipped his hand lower past Elana's until he reached the bottom band of the sweatshirt she wore. Bunching it up in his hand, he worked the shirt up, exposing flesh rubbing against his knuckles. Warm, soft, vulnerable flesh. Elana didn't suck her stomach in, scoot back or break off their kiss. She pressed her hand on his and moved her hand lower, copying his actions until her knuckles touched his belly. Tickling his navel slightly as she worked the sweatshirt higher. Elana pressed tight to him. They lay flesh to flesh, kissing and enjoying the cocoon of passion and warmth enveloping them.

James broke off the kiss. "Wow, I think we stoked the fire for sure."

. "Agreed." Elana winked and kissed him again. "Do we want to shuck shirts? Get fully naked?"

"Depends on how quickly things cool off." James let a pocket of air into their cocoon covers.

"That is chilly." Elana shook her head. "Fun begins with trying to get enough of the shirts off under the covers."

James laughed. "Reminds me of the time we went camping and the damn zipper on the double sleeping bag stuck. Wiggling in and out of it. Trying to keep our clothes on doing that."

"We could wrestle each other like we did our first night here." Elana snickered.

"Yeah and end up with one of those free-for-all tag team events we used to watch on TV as kids. The covers, the sweatshirts and us." James slid the sleeve off his arm closest to Elana. "Need help getting a sleeve off?"

"No. I can do that myself." Elana shoved the empty sleeve out from under the covers. "Remember how many times it took us to get out of that blasted sleeping bag and still have our clothes on?"

James snorted. "Yeah, and one of those practice runs our parents snuck up on us."

Elana grinned, nodding. "Got both of us double chores and grounded for a week."

"Right before a full moon." James snuggled closer. "Half morphed and trying to explain, thinking I scared you off."

"You ducked behind the closest bush." Elana pulled her other empty sleeve out from under the covers. "One of my fondest memories, you covered in calamine lotion trying not to scratch the poison ivy welts."

"Your fondest memory?" James waved his second empty sleeve at Elana.

"You kissed me, told me you were a wolf shifter and jumped back." Elana pressed against James. "I snapped my fingers, said a short incantation and a wand appeared in my hand."

"I called you a witch." James slipped his hand lower, brushing his fingers through Elana's pubic hair. "You called me a pink wolf."

"Well you were. Calamine lotion is pink." Elana clasped James's cock and squeezed lightly. "Even your cock was a lovely pink hue. It did like my kisses that day."

"Still does darling. Still does." James lightly traced the v of Elana's vulva. "I remember your perky nipples and your clitoris matching their rosy hue."

Elana trembled. James dipped two fingers into the v of her mons, coating the tips with Elana's wetness. Across and over her taut clitoris, he traced as he cupped her breast closest to him. Slowly, he dragged his tongue over the nipple tip until it rose, brushing against his lips, begging for more attention.

"Delicious being with you this way," James murmured.

"Agreed." Elana cupped James's balls. Carefully palming them as she continued speaking. "We didn't get far our first night here. I think we need to talk before we do more."

James sighed and started to remove his hand.

"No need for that." Elana squeezed her legs together. "Do we need condoms? Sexual health discussion?"

James nodded, sliding his hand back to its prior position, cupping Elana's mons as his fingers teased her clitoris. "I doubt either of us can get pregnant at our age."

Elana snickered. "You for sure. As to me, through menopause and well past fertile."

James brushed his lips over Elana's. "Good to know. Sexual health disclosure. No STDs. General health checkup two months ago. Sexually inactive by choice. Wanting more than momentary thrills."

"I understand." Elana let go of James's balls. She lightly gripped James's cock with her hand. Squeezing as she stroked upwards. "Got a checkup a month ago. No STDs either. Gynecologist asked why I wanted tested. Said healthy body creates a healthy peace of mind."

"Darlin' sounds like we're deciding to move forward on being lovers." James suckled her nipple into his mouth, flicked his tongue over it rapidly and let go. "If you want to use condoms, I'm on board. Protecting you is important to me."

"Celibate, other than my battery-operated boyfriend for last several years." Elana slipped her leg between James's. "Personal choice. I'm a lover. Not a one-night stand doer."

"Thanks for sharing, Elana." James cupped Elana's face between his hands. "What about condoms? Do we or don't we?"

"Two things are happening here." Elana paused, making sure she had James's attention. His gaze met hers. "We're fluid bonding and—becoming friends with benefits."

James pressed tighter to Elana. "Something bigger than that."

"Bigger?"

"Yes," James began. "Lovers."

Elana draped her leg over his hip, rocking toward him. On her next rock tight to him, she guided him into her and stopped moving. "Lovers it is. Caring, best friend lovers."

James brushed his lips over Elana's, placing his hands on her hips. "Yes, the best combination."

Neither looked away. Hands and lips met, steering each where they wanted and needed them to be. James thrust forward, holding still. "Deep within your warmth. Nirvana for this old wolf."

Elana kissed him. "Not old. A wolf that has much to give and cares for those important to him."

Sighs and soft murmurs continued as passion and desire compounded. James slipped his fingers lower into Elana's vulva. Wetness greeted him, slicking his fingertips. Up, around, over and across, he trailed his fingers as he captured Elana's nipple between his teeth. He nipped and laved the taut nipple, flicking his tongue over it rapidly, mimicking what his fingers were doing to her clitoris.

"So close." Elana groaned, grasping his shoulders. "So so close."

James suckled Elana's nipple more as he stroked his fingers quickly over her clitoris. Jerks and shudders tightened her around him. He rocked his hips in counter rhythm to her movement. In and out, back and forth until—"I'm there!"

His balls tightened, swelling. One seismic ripple after another ignited, boiling upwards. Bright bursts of green, marine blue and aqua lit his subconscious where his wolf and he blended. Where his two halves became one. His lips parted. A low growl began deep inside him. Building in intensity until his head tipped back and a joyous howl sounded. Muffled by the blankets, the howl reverberated through him, claiming and appeasing his wolf simultaneously.

His vision cleared. Elana gazed at him, her lips moving. The words he caught wormed their way into his heart. Joy, cherish, and contentment. What joyous adjectives. He hoped Elana murmured a blessing.

Elana blew him a kiss. "You are a cherished contentment that fills my heart with joy."

Moments of contented quiet and enjoyment passed as they lay replete in each other's arms. Elana reached for the blanket and sheet, ready to cover her and James.

A hard knock followed by a ratatat sounded on the door. "Aunt Elana? James?" Siobhan asked as she cracked open the door. "Ty's cooking breakfast. Will you be joining us?"

TWENTY

James stifled a yawn. He glanced at Elana and nodded.

"We'll join you in a bit." Elana quickly slid her arms into the sweatshirt sleeves.

"There's some hot water. Might want to conserve it by showering together." Siobhan's titter faded as she latched the door.

"Don't like being told what to do." James sat up, chafing his arms. "*But...*"

Elana laughed. "As long as it's fun, you *might* do it."

"Hey, fun is worth doing. Don't you agree?" James leaned over and kissed her cheek. "I'm all for conservation. Especially when it comes to doing it with you darlin'."

Elana held up both hands. "I call dibs on the hot water. You can wait your turn, you know."

"Ah, like hell I am." James tossed the covers off, shucked his sweatshirt and trotted toward the bathroom. "Too damn cold to argue over who goes first. Together, it is. Not like we ain't seen each other buckassed naked before."

Elana stood, pulled off her sweatshirt and hastily made her way to the bathroom. "It's nude, James. It's nude."

"Aye. We are that too." The sound of the toilet flushing greeted her as she entered the bathroom. James spun around, shook his hips at her, grinned and stepped into the shower. "Come on. The conserving needs happening now."

Ten minutes passed while they soaped and rinsed. James exited the shower first. He grabbed the first towel, hurriedly drying off. "Beats a sponge bath.

Coordinating who washed what on who took more thought than I am ready for."

Elana turned the shower off and pulled back the curtain. "Bs, James. You loved running your soapy hands all over me."

"Not denying it, sweetie." James grinned, handing her a towel. "We got our hair washed. Our essentials and managed to rinse all in a few minutes."

"Didn't help I had to turn the shower off as a blast of cold water came out of the tap." Elana started drying off.

James shrugged, grinning. "French kissing does, uhmm—distract the mind, you know."

"Short distraction. You better put some clothes on or those goosebumps might overwhelm you." Elana wrapped the towel around her and moved past James into the bedroom.

Elana tossed the sweatshirt James slept in at him. "Best put this on and something to cover your nethers. Shrivelling things up might cause a chill."

She swiftly put on her bra and panties, followed by jeans and the sweatshirt she slept in. As she tied her shoes, James sat down beside her and began putting his shoes on. "If things are too shriveled, a few well-placed kisses will warm things up."

"*We'll*," Elana began, standing up, "have to see about that later."

James grimaced, keeping his gaze directed on his shoes. Elana's emphasis on we sounded a bit acerbic. Elana's shoes came into view. He looked up as she patted his shoulder. "Not scolding you. Just stressing it's gonna take both of us to warm things up if they're too chilled and shriveled."

Elana winked and exited the bedroom. James tied his shoes and stood. He knew better than trying to decipher what someone else meant before his second cup of coffee. Heck, even before his first, he had trouble translating his own muddled, half-asleep thoughts. Where he had been in the last hour or so needed distraction and a hearty breakfast plus a large cup of coffee.

As Elana crossed the living room, she caught bits and pieces of Ty and Siobhan's conversation.

"Ty, are you sure you want to do the test now?" Siobhan's voice squeaked on now.

Elana paused, not sure how to announce her presence without interrupting them.

"Siobhan, it doesn't matter when today, we do the test." Ty paced across the kitchen. Not looking out toward the living room as he continued speaking. "The test needs done. Sure, the sooner, the better. It's not like we're going anywhere anytime soon until the storm lets up."

Siobhan walked up behind Ty and turned. She gawked at Elana, put her hand over her mouth and nudged Ty hard with her elbow.

"Good morning, Aunt Elana." Siobhan nudged Ty again.

"Morning Elana." Ty glanced at Siobhan, shaking his head.

"I'm deflating the balloon in the room." Elana moved forward. "No need to let stuff morph into elephants or boulders."

"I miss something?" James asked, coming up behind her.

"Ty and Siobhan were having a private discussion." Elana held her hand out to James. "They aren't sure about when to do the pregnancy test."

"Sorry, Aunt Elana." Siobhan began, dropping down on the couch. "Didn't mean to drag you and James into this."

Ty sat down beside Siobhan. "I'm apologizing too."

James squeezed Elana's hand and let go. "No apology needed for me."

"Same here." Elana sat in the chair across from the couch. James perched on the arm next to her. "We're already involved. When the test occurs isn't our concern."

"Elana's right." James rose. "We're here for you regardless of the test results."

"Thanks James." Siobhan faced Ty, adding. "Aunt Elana, Ty and I appreciate you being involved. You too, James."

"Siobhan," Elana said, standing. "The test can wait. Food and coffee first. Decisions once we're all on the same page, okay?"

Siobhan walked over to her, hugged her tight and stepped back. "Ty, is that
omelet of yours done? The pancakes ready? I warmed the syrup."

"Bacon is ready. Coffee made." Ty stood and stretched. "I could use time for my brain to catch up with the rest of me."

Siobhan laughed. "I think all of us are ready for coffee and breakfast."

Elana entered the kitchen. Delicious scents greeted her. Freshly brewed drip coffee. Maple syrup next as she approached the counter, reaching for the plates and utensils. Bacon, extra crispy, sat on the microwave crisping tray freshly cooked. She picked up the plates, turning toward the table. Four mugs, sugar bowl and carton of half-and-half sat center of the table. A family meal ready for partaking. Yet, not family completely. Choice mattered and they'd made those choices last night. Uniting together. Not just because of a possible pregnancy. United because they cared about each other and chose to be family of blood and choice.

James pulled out a chair and sat down. "How can I help? Besides getting out of the way."

Elana smirked, placing the plates and utensils in front of him. "Put these around the table. I'll pour the coffee. You might try drinking straight from the pot."

James handed Ty a plate and utensils as he sat down next to him. "Elana honey, the only thing I drink straight from the pot is you."

Siobhan rapped on the table. "Before I shout TMI, how about you two settle down?"

"Oh, you mean behave?" Elana filled the first mug with coffee and set it on the table next to where Siobhan stood.

Siobhan picked up the mug, sipped and replied. "Yes."

James laughed, taking the mug Elana held out to him. "Siobhan, sorry for the embarrassment. But kids don't always listen."

"He's not saying we don't hear you." Elana pushed a full mug across the table to Ty.

Ty sipped his coffee twice and rose. "Siobhan, please relax. I'll get the food. We're family here. No need for you to take on hostess role, okay?"

Siobhan pulled out a chair and sat down. She cupped her hands around her mug of coffee and sighed. "Sorry everyone. I'm nervous about taking the test."

"Hon, I know not knowing is egging us both." Ty handed her a plate with pancakes, some omelet, and bacon. "Are you unsure you want the baby?"

Siobhan set the plate down with a thud. "Not want the baby?"

Elana put her mug down and set the empty coffee carafe in the sink. "Pause for a moment, okay?"

"Aunt Elana, I've been pausing. Pushing my thoughts aside. I'm sure one moment. Unsure the next." Siobhan buttered and syruped her pancakes. "I wish I could make up my mind."

"I'm gonna say something that might sound out of line." James laid his hand on Siobhan's arm. "What are you more afraid of? Being a parent or the letdown if you aren't pregnant?"

Siobhan gripped her fork, speared part of the omelet and held the fork up. "Nothing is crystal clear. I don't want to end up like my parents. Constantly bickering. Throwing out barbs and jibs about the reason they married was because Mom got knocked up."

"Siobhan, there's something you don't know about your parents." Elana sat down next to Siobhan. "Only a few family members knew. I'm going to tell you about it. Maybe you'll understand better why your parents needed to split up but refused to follow their own advice."

Elana glanced around the table. Ty, James and Siobhan's gaze met hers. What she was about to say was a deep family secret that some swore to take with them to the beyond. Thank goodness she wasn't one of them.

She sipped her coffee and settled back against the chair. Finding the words to start the conversation eluded her. Jumping into the story event wasn't going to make sense. Every time she thought about telling Siobhan, question and answer was the one way it all made sense. The tale had to start at some point.

Elana slowly exhaled, wet her lips and spoke. "Please hear me out before you ask too many questions."

Siobhan nodded.

"When your parents met, interspecies dating, mixing, even mingling was forbidden. Supernatural rules and so-called etiquette forbade it. Purity of lineage plus species was the primal order. Surviving meant taking care of your own." Elana clasped James's hand. "James and I were part of the youth that met covertly. We knew if we were to survive, we had to depend on each other. Species or magical abilities wasn't going to keep families, towns or generations alive."

"Isn't this part of the Great Reveal's history?" Ty asked. "Sorry, I interrupted."

"It's okay, Ty." Elana ate two bites of her omelet and swallowed. "Being mortal, you know bits and pieces."

Ty held up his hand. "Before you go on, I'm part mortal. My family can trace their shape shifter bloodlines back to before the Reveal and Caleb is my cousin."

"You mean—" Siobhan's mouth moved, no words came out. She sat gawking at him.

"Yes, I am a mixed breed too. Magic is not my thing unless you count the sleight of hand I can do sometimes. More the sniff things out type with intuition and keen cunning, aka as my mom used to say, lots of smarts." Ty brushed his lips over Siobhan's.

"Our child could be a mixed mixture." Siobhan turned to Elana. "How much crap is this going to stir up?"

Elana smiled and shrugged. "There's been a few standouts like Caleb whose matchmaking abilities peaked early on during his teen years."

"Yes, Caleb was setting up couples and counseling them throughout high school." Ty nudged Siobhan. "Eat while the food is hot. We can discuss peculiarities later."

Siobhan glared at him. He winked and blew her a kiss. "Stop worrying. This child will get lots of love, affection and, if needed, protection."

Siobhan started eating, glancing at her aunt from time to time. Was she going to finish her tale or not?

TWENTY-ONE

Elana laid her fork and knife down and wiped her mouth. James refilled everyone's mugs with fresh coffee. The muffins he quickly mixed up from the various items he found in Siobhan's cabinets and pantry cooled on top of the stove. A fresh pot of coffee sat on the counter.

"Rate we're going with munching out, we're going to have to raid Siobhan's chest freezer." Elana rubbed her hands together. "We might have to draw straws to see who's going to brave the snow and wind to do that."

"Why would we do that? Chest freezer out in the woods?" James set a plate holding muffins on the table.

Siobhan pointed at the patio doors. "Styrofoam ice chests. Far corner of the patio. Wind reaches there and is the coldest spot."

James arched an eyebrow, stuck out his tongue and gazed at the patio doors. "What you got out there that wouldn't be better off in an electric freezer?"

Ty quickly set his mug down. "Siobhan, if you don't tell him, I will."

"Come on, Ty. James was all set to tackle the job," Siobhan quipped.

"Freeze vital parts of my furry arse or human sexiness?" James shook his head. "Ain't happening unless there's a damn fine reason to even contemplate it."

Siobhan covered her mouth. Elana snorted and snickered. "James, what is that appliance between the fridge and counter?"

James got up, walked over to the large white chest, thumped it and peeked inside. "All descriptions say chest freezer."

"I think we've gotten that figured out." Siobhan stood, hugged James and sat next to her aunt. "Aunt Elana, enough distractions. What about my parents?"

"Some will deny this. Others may act surprised." Elana turned in her chair and faced Siobhan. "Your mom and dad had to get married."

"I know this." Siobhan bit into one of the muffins James made. She chewed and washed it down with coffee.

"What you don't know is why they had to get married." Elana broke a piece off the muffin close to her, popped it in her mouth and chewed. She wiped her fingers on her napkin. "They were chosen as one of the experimental couples."

"Shit, I'd forgotten about that." James set his empty mug on the table.

"Experimental couples? Aunt Elana, what are you talking about?"

"Siobhan, quite a few believe that interspecies mating couldn't produce offspring." Elana held her mug out to James as he filled his mug with part of the remaining coffee.

"Science doesn't lie." Ty placed their empty plates in the sink. "Except we're an anomaly. Dual natures that none were sure what would result."

"Correct, Ty." Elana toyed with her napkin. "What I'm telling is documented in older studies conducted when the decision to see what would happen when interspecies married and mated. Siobhan, your parents entered their names in the lottery for the preliminary couples. As children of alpha and beta leaders, no one expected their names would be chosen."

"If I remember right from what I read," James began, "they were fifth pair up chosen. No way leaders on either side could step in or get them disqualified."

"Yeah, and their rival clans were chuckling and jeering. See Siobhan, your great great granddads and great great grandmas were feuding for over a hundred years. Land rights. Magical vs. supernatural. The list was constantly under revision about claims and wrong doings. Then your grandparents on both sides signed a peace treaty of sorts." Elana finished her muffin and coffee.

Siobhan stood up. "Why am I just hearing about this now?"

"Because vows of silence aren't meant to be broken." James cleared the rest of the brunch dishes off the table and handed them to Ty.

"Are you referring to the Honored Silence?" Ty squirted dish detergent on the dishes and filled the sink with hot water.

"Yes. How do you know about it?" James spread a dish towel on the counter, set the dish drainer and rack on it.

"Supernatural police training 101." Ty washed and rinsed the plates and utensils. "Understanding why solid evidence was the only thing we have to go on is essential to maintaining respect and the balance of the factions' cohesion."

"Aunt Elana, go on with what you were saying." Siobhan wiped off the table.

"Siobhan, you best sit down for the rest of this." Elana pulled out the chair next to her. "It's the hard part of the story."

Siobhan, James and Ty sat at the table. Their attention focused on Elana.

"Your parents married and mated because they wanted and had to. Others of the experimental couples did as well. Your parents figured after they produced a few offspring, regardless of whether they were magical or supernatural, they could part ways."

Ty laid his hand on Siobhan's. Elana's gaze met James's. He nodded and blew her a kiss. The next few words could make or break Siobhan's resolve, heart and her inner peace.

"This is the hard part of the story. The part that wasn't officially recorded in the Great Reveal records. It's hinted at in the Honored Silence. The records were sealed and hidden deep within a cavern beneath City Hall. Only a few know of its existence and how to find the cavern." Elana stood and began pacing, tapping her fingers against her leg as she paced.

"Elana, are you sure you want to go on?" James caught her hand as she paced by the table.

"Yes. Siobhan needs to know." Elana dropped into her chair. "Siobhan, your parents were among the first couples to get pregnant. Miscarriages happened. People claimed this was evidence that magical and supernaturals were genetically incompatible. Some couples gave up and waited out the required mating period before breaking up."

Siobhan nodded and motioned for her to continue.

"Your parents tried again, figuring it was their duty as leaders' children. Two more miscarriages followed. Your grandparents on both sides submitted a petition to allow for early dissolution of their match. As the date for the dissolution ruling approached, your mother found out she was three months pregnant. The matchmakers' council and the Reveal council ruled your parents weren't eligible for a dissolution."

"Mom said she was stuck with Dad. Stuck until the bitter end. She didn't know I overheard her cursing her fertility each time she got pregnant. They played us kids against the parent we didn't side with. Played us against each other from time to time. Lupa, no wonder I ran when I was old enough."

Siobhan sniffled. Wiped a tear off her cheek and faced Ty. "If I am pregnant, our child is not going through that. I want this child. Our child."

Ty hugged Siobhan and faced Elana. "I am bearing witness in front of you in your official matchmaker capacity with James as a witness. I will not deny my child, nor will I neglect my child and his or her mother."

"Thank you, Ty." Siobhan placed both hands on the table and stood. "I'm not expecting you to marry me. We'll discuss more once we know the pregnancy test results."

"Siobhan, I'm sorry you had to learn about this this way." Elana hugged Siobhan and stepped away. "Your parents lusted after each other every full moon unless your mom was pregnant. By the time, your youngest sister was born, several other mixed-breed children populated the growing space nicknamed Cauldron Falls. Cuz everyone said nothing falls far from the cauldron."

"It's okay, Aunt Elana." Siobhan rummaged in one of the plastic bags sitting on the counter. "I think it's time for the test. Time to know whether a product of Ty's and my caring and loving is nestled inside me."

"Siobhan, I'll go with you." Ty started following her.

"Don't need that kind of help, Ty. Thanks for offering." Siobhan turned. "Peeing on a stick or in a paper cup, I can handle by myself."

Ty returned to the table and sat between James and Elana. He slumped down in the chair. "What do I do now?"

"Wait, son. Wait." James patted Ty's shoulder. "Patience is a virtue. Sometimes we got to create our own patient virtue."

Elana started drying the remaining dishes in the dish drainer. "Let's keep busy. Watching the clock or bathroom door isn't going to make things happen any faster."

Siobhan clicked the bathroom door shut. She laid the pregnancy test package on the counter. The instructions said she could pee on the stick or dip it in a cup of her urine. She glanced at the instructions, reading the last instruction line twice. "Dip tip in collected urine for 10 seconds. Recap and lay flat. Wait 2 to 3 minutes for results to appear."

Thankful she didn't have an audience or Ty waiting outside the door, Siobhan lowered her jeans and underwear, sat on the toilet and let nature take its course. She placed the quarter-full cup on the counter and finished up.

As Siobhan stood, a past thought and image flashed through her mind. The small four-bedroom cottage-style home was all her parents could afford. One bathroom for four kids and two adults led to some hilarious sharing times and a few almost knock-down drag-out fights as her brothers got older and didn't want to share anymore. The half bath her parents built into one corner of their bedroom served as the overflow if one of them had to go right now. Lines outside the bathroom were part of making your way through the hall into the main part of the house. Praise Lupa, her condo had two full baths and a half bath. One key reason she bought the condo.

She washed and dried her hands. Her hands shook as she picked up the test package. Opening it, dipping the test tip in the urine, she was ready to do. Waiting the two to three minutes she wasn't so sure about. She opened the package, gripped the test stick, slowly exhaled and uncapped the test stick. Placing the tip in the urine, she sang the first verse and chorus from one of her favorite childhood songs. Round the bush, the children circled and picked flowers to make bouquets until they all fell down.

She picked up the cap, glanced at the testing stick, slowly exhaled and glided the cap on. A soft click sounded, indicating the seal was in place. Waiting had started. Siobhan discarded the remaining urine and tossed the cup in the trash. She washed and dried her hands again. By the time, she opened the door and let the others know results were forthcoming, the answer would be there. Was she ready to know? Ready to share with the others? Tell them all together or. . .She had to get out of the bathroom. Pacing in cramped places gave her the heebie-jeebies.

TWENTY-TWO

Ty stood the moment he heard the bathroom door open. Helping Elana and James clean up the kitchen had distracted him some. James's attempt at funny stories and jokes had Elana begging him to stop with the kid knock-knock jokes and tales from their junior high and high school days. Elana had gone into her and James's bedroom to collect laundry and asked if he and Siobhan had any. Ty almost blurted out how could two people have dirty clothes when they slept naked. . .well almost naked. Long-sleeved gender-neutral sleep shirts that barely covered either his or Siobhan's ass probably weren't dirty. What clothes he did have with him in his duffle were from his gym locker and the two extra sets of clothes he kept at work. Washing everything would ensure he had clean clothes for the next few days.

"I'll get my stuff in a moment, Elana." Ty closed the space between him and Siobhan. "Well?"

Siobhan sidestepped around Ty. "In a few moments, okay. I need some space. And something sweet. Any muffins left?"

"Sure are." James got up off the couch. "I'm coffeed out. I saw some loose-leaf chamomile tea in one of the cabinets. Can make some in the coffee maker."

"Good idea." Siobhan moved further away from Ty. "Please go help James. I need to talk to Aunt Elana for a couple minutes."

Ty glanced at James. James shrugged and entered the kitchen. Ty glanced at Siobhan again. Her back was to him. Antsy and wanting to know what was going on barely touched where his thoughts went. He slowly unclenched his hands, shoved them in his jeans pockets and followed James into the kitchen.

"Elana," James began as he refilled the coffee maker with water. "Siobhan needs you."

"I heard." Elana kissed his cheek as she moved past him. "It's not about you or Ty. Give us a few minutes."

Elana exited the kitchen. Siobhan sat on the arm of the chair closest to the bathroom. Elana knew that posture. Struggling to remain strong. Wanting to circle into herself and shut the world out. Siobhan had taken on the role of both her parents when her siblings came to live with her once she had custody of them. Another small person was going to need her parenting skills. Siobhan's gaze met hers as Elana perched on the other arm of the chair facing Siobhan.

"You know the results." Elana opened her arms, ready to hug Siobhan. Mothering wasn't easy. This time she would be the parent. Not the oldest sibling trying to be all and still have a teenage life. Growing up fast wasn't a skill any schooling or textbook readily taught. Parenting herself hadn't been easy on Siobhan either.

"Not officially. " Siobhan flashed a weak grin. "Gut instinct. You know that nagging feeling that refuses to let go."

"I sure do. One of the strongest psychic traits our family possesses. Not an easy one to ignore. Do you need a hug?"

Siobhan nodded. "I sure do. I hugged me twice. Tried to center doing the quick meditation you taught me. Look out a window. Focus on an object in the distance and slowly inhale and exhale. Count to a thousand by twos."

"Not much to focus on with ice and snow covering most of the window." Elana slid off the arm of the chair and into it. She wrapped both arms around Siobhan as she leaned into the hug. "My lap doesn't hold much anymore. You're welcome to sit for a bit."

Siobhan straightened, smiling. "No, what I need is to face what the test results are. I'm not alone in this. Ty, James and you are here with me."

Elana nodded. "Let's get the muffins and tea in here. Then we all go into the bathroom together to find out the official results."

"Hope we all fit." Siobhan moved toward the kitchen. "Thank Lupa, I am not claustrophobic."

James placed the carafe of chamomile tea, mugs, and honey pot on the coffee table. "Ty's got the muffins, spoons and napkins."

Ty set the muffins, spoons and napkins down. "How long does it take for the test results to appear?"

Siobhan opened the bathroom door. "Two to three minutes. I know it's been longer than that."

"Hope that won't invalidate the results." Ty stepped into the bathroom, turned and exited. "Siobhan, you should go in first."

Siobhan shrugged. "My test. I get to see the results first."

Elana nudged James and pointed to Ty.

James moved closer and whispered. "Ty, let Siobhan lead."

Ty nodded and faced Siobhan, holding out his hand. "How do you want to do this?"

"This is my reveal. I'm leading." Siobhan squeezed Ty's hand, let go and entered the bathroom. She faced Elana, James and Ty, who stood outside the door. "Come on in. It's time for the results reveal."

James, Elana and Ty formed a semi-circle around Siobhan as she lifted the test stick from the cup. She carefully grasped the stick's middle and held it up to the overhead lights. Her hand shook the closer she brought the stick to her. She swallowed hard. Blinked and lowered the stick.

"Ty, you need to see this." Siobhan held the stick where Ty could see over her shoulder. He reached out, clasping her wrist.

"I-I'm gonna." Ty didn't say more. Elana glanced at their mirrored reflections. Ty's mouth hung open. His gaze darted from the test to Siobhan and back to the test.

"Yes, we're gonna be parents." Siobhan slipped her wrist out of Ty's grip. "Maybe Aunt Elana and James would like to see the results."

"James and I saw." Elana hugged Siobhan briefly. "James, grab the pad and pen off the fridge. I'm sure there's going to be questions and notes to write down."

Elana followed James out of the bathroom, leaving Siobhan and Ty in there.

Ty pressed his lips together, inhaling and counting as a sentence echoed through his thoughts: *I'm going to be a dad*. Being a dad was something he'd given a lot of thought to. He hadn't figured it happening for a while.

"Ty, are you all right?" Siobhan tossed the test kit packing in the trash.

"For the most part, yeah." Ty leaned against the counter, facing Siobhan. "How you doing?"

"Shocked, scared, and dismayed." Siobhan picked up the test stick. "I knew, before I did the test, I probably was pregnant. Knowing for sure, puts it in a different aspect. It's here and real. Very real according to this."

"Very real for both of us." Ty straightened. "How far along do you think you are?"

"Not sure. Maybe six to eight weeks." Siobhan stepped around him, tossing the test stick in the trash.

Ty glanced at the stick sitting on top of the crumpled urine cup. Part of him wanted to grab the stick and stash it away. Evidence he could produce life. Evidence his family would. . .Ah hell, his family would scoff, debride him about being careless since he was the mutt of the pack according to them. His magic cousins welcomed him with standoffishness. Caleb and a few other cousins embraced who they were. Didn't matter if magic or supernatural shape shifting dominated their genes. Accepting and supporting each other was their primary concern.

Ty sat next to Siobhan on the couch. "Did you make the appointment with Doc McAdams?"

"Yes." Siobhan slumped down against the arm of the couch. "His service called to confirm yesterday morning. In a couple days, we'll have the official medical prognosis."

"James and I can go with you and Ty. Be moral support," Elana offered.

"Thanks, Aunt Elana. I appreciate the offer." Siobhan sat up. "I don't think it's necessary. Can we talk about something else? Take my mind off this for a while."

"I got a text from my new neighbors. They checked my place from top to bottom. Heat was on. No pipes frozen. Water running." Elana filled all the mugs with tea. "I almost didn't buy the townhouse."

"What changed your mind?" James took a mug from her and handed it to Ty.

"The other places I considered were too far from Siobhan." Elana handed Siobhan a mug. "I've reached a point where being closer to family and friends is what I want. Living alone is okay to a point."

"Boy, do I know that one." James passed the plate of muffins to everyone. "That's one of the reasons I came home for the holidays this year. Thinking maybe it's time to consider moving."

Ty picked up the TV remote. "How about a movie? We've got a couple of hours until dinner time."

"There's several Christmas specials and movies to choose from." Siobhan flipped through the program guide. "How about this one? A single mother and her three children move into their new apartment on Christmas Eve. Her single next-door neighbor invites them to Christmas Eve dinner. Can a four-star single Chef and an uprising business CEO find their Christmas present where they least expect it?"

James guffawed. "Sounds like Maggie and Caleb, if you ask me?'

Elana groaned. "I don't know who if I want to cheer one of them on or feel sorry."

Ty snickered. "Lupa and the One probably figured they were a great match. Both are stubborn to a point. Don't put up with crap. And are attracted to each other."

"Between their auras and pheromones—let's watch the movie." Siobhan grabbed the remote from Ty.

Ty glanced from James to Elana. They both nodded, grinning. Hot auras and pheromones definitely permeated the air last night. How had Caleb and Maggie fared the storm? Cooped up together for two whole days and nights. Had their smoldering pheromones sparked both of them into a passionate bonfire?

TWENTY-THREE

C aleb rolled over, reaching for the pillow bundle middle of the bed. Flesh. Bare naked flesh. *What?*

"Warm up your hand," Maggie muttered, snuggling closer to him.

Maggie snuggled closer to him? He opened one eye, blinked, and quickly shielded his eyes against the sunlight streaming in through the partially open blinds.

Cold air shot under the blanket and sheet, icing its way down him. His cock tightened against him. He was naked. Bareassed naked in bed with Maggie who was. . .Caleb clutched the top edge of the sheet. Did he look under it? Confirm what his psyche kept flashing pictures of? He and Maggie passionately having sex?

"Uhm, I got a question." Caleb glanced to where Maggie lay on her side, covers pulled up to her neck.

Maggie blinked, squinted, and yawned. "Yeah."

"When, how—no, not how."

Maggie tittered. "You showed you know how last night."

Caleb bolted upright, wrapping the covers around him as best he could. "You double-dared me."

"I dared you to kiss me once. Figured it would be quick and get it out of the way since you kept hinting at it for the last two days. Once wasn't apparently enough." Maggie stretched. "You're damn fine kisser. And a fantabulous lover. Best sleep I've had in months. I don't need new batteries for my vibrator with you around."

"Birth control?"

"Didn't count how many condoms we used. As long as the last one didn't spring a leak, you're safe. I mean we're safe." Maggie tossed the covers off, rose, and stretched fully in view of him.

Caleb gulped. What in Lupa and the One's name had he gotten himself into? His cock thickened. Warmth rushed over him as Maggie turned and bent over. Lush view and memories of her plump behind filling his hands as he filled her from behind.

He jumped out of bed, rushed out of the room, and slammed the bathroom door closed. A cold shower wasn't what he needed. A bucket of ice-cold water wasn't going to douse the fire going on deep within his groin and heart.

"Love spark caught you, eh?" His psyche could shut up.

"Why should I? I'm you and you know this is where you wanted to be. You met one that gave as good as you. Your control and I enjoyed the doings as much as you."

Caleb turned on the shower and stepped in. He needed a hot shower and food plus coffee before he thought about last night more. His spur-of-the-moment match and supposed chaperoning weren't turning out quite like he'd. . .planned? A knock rattled the bathroom door. Another knock sounded as the door clicked open.

Maggie called out as she opened the door. "Caleb, hiding out in the shower isn't going to work when you run out of hot water. Cut the temp back, please. I'd like to shower too."

Caleb picked up the soap, worked up a lather and peeked around the shower curtain. Empty. The bathroom was empty. Just him, the steaming shower, and the bloody open door. Maybe Maggie respected a man's shower time. He quietly laughed. They tried to discuss other things. Damn lust kept revving its umph up and . . . Lupa, he hoped that was out of their systems for a bit. A bit being longer than twenty-four hours.

Maggie stepped into her shower, quickly soaping and rinsing. Caleb's scramble away from her raised questions. She had a few answers. They'd driven each other nuts with puns and innuendos. Taunts and rants a few times as well. The last man she'd had this connection with walked away. Left her standing at the justice of the peace. Left her having to explain to his family and her friends what happened. Thank Lupa and the One her so-called parents—left her with cousins and hadn't come back for years—weren't alive to witness that. Caleb's personal honor was at stake if he did the same thing. Both of their matchmaking reputations were at stake. They knew what others said about each of them. Nothing either of them could build much around except the lusty attraction. As she dried off, Maggie sent a quick prayer up. The last couple of days she'd felt more secure than she had in a long time. Safer and securer. How deep was her heart in this?

Caleb looked down at the frilly purple apron tied around his waist. He was up to elbows in sudsy water washing his and Maggie's breakfast and dinner dishes. Potluck meals didn't require a menu. It required on-the-spot ingenuity. Maggie whipped up a batch of biscuits and sausage gravy for breakfast. Her next-door neighbor brought over a dozen eggs his chickens laid. Helping the man shovel Maggie's and his driveways reminded Caleb of the camaraderie he and his cousins had when they got together. Helping each other was one of their main ways of taking care of each other and the community they lived in. Sylvan Valley flourished because everyone looked out for each other. There was something about small towns where you knew your neighbors' name and they yours.

"Maggie, what are you doing?" Caleb rolled his eyes, knowing he'd probably asked a stupid question.

"Figuring out if I attack you now or later." Maggie's laughter reached Caleb as he dried his hands and walked toward the living room. "Good enough answer?"

Caleb shook his head, tossed the dish towel on the table and reached behind him to untie the damn blasted apron Maggie had insisted he wear. That she double fracking knotted! How the hell was he supposed to get the damn thing off?

"Stop fussing with the knot. I knew you were going to try to take it off." Maggie entered the kitchen. "Turn around. I goaded you good."

Caleb counted, pressed each finger and thumb of both hands against his leg, and looked up. He hoped he wore his best tacky smile. "Perhaps not. I usually. . ." Caleb's voice trailed off. He winked as Maggie's gaze met his, blew her a kiss and pulled a chair out from the table. "Why don't you entertain me with what your attack plan is, darlin'?"

"You know Caleb, we could keep these verbal banters up or have a real discussion about why me and you?" Maggie tossed the pad she held on the table.

"Let me think about this." Caleb sat in the chair he pulled out. "One, a cold zipper in my face most of the night. Two, you insisted on the bundle pile middle of the bed. Kept snatching the covers off both of us if either of us turned over. We spent half the night cuddling it when we could have been cuddling a few of the pillows between us and been warmer. Do you need me to go on?"

Maggie sat across from him. "Let me continue for you. Three, you had to eat my cooking. Not that you complained much until after you had seconds. Four, you offered to do the dishes and lost the bet about the apron when I came up with the recipe for lunch. Do *you* need me to go on?"

"All right. We're at an impasse." Caleb stood, walked over to Maggie and turned. "Will you please unknot this damn thing?"

Maggie laughed. "Sure, if you're certain you don't want to continue your exquisite look."

Caleb spun around, placed both hands on the back of Maggie's chair, and leaned down until her breath rushed across his face. "No, I'd rather do this."

Maggie tried to stand. "You wouldn't."

Caleb cupped Maggie's face, inching closer until their noses almost touched. "I would and am, darlin'. I am."

He tilted his head and leaned forward until his lips and Maggie's met. He traced the top edge of her bottom lip with his tongue. Captured it between his teeth, nibbled slightly and let go. Caleb lowered his hands, straightened and stepped back. "Next time you want to kiss me. Just ask. I'm very willing to accommodate you."

Maggie rubbed the back of her hand across her lips. "Why would I want to do that?"

"Pheromones." Caleb turned, smiling. "Remember my shape shifter blood? I can smell your desire plus your delicious aura turns red and yellow every time I get near you."

Maggie slumped in the chair. Shit, she'd been caught. Why had she skipped pheromone masking class? Withdrew from aura reading basics? So much for leveling the playing field. Score Caleb four, Maggie two. And the weather forecaster said the storm wouldn't break until tomorrow. Lupa, help them.

TWENTY-FOUR

Siobhan reached in her pocket for her keys. Two days ago, she'd found out unofficially she was pregnant. Tomorrow was Solstice. A day of celebration and preparation for the new year. A time of reflection and change. Celebrations included family and friends who welcomed the passing of the torch by the moon to the sun. The dawning of a new phase of life. And hers was phasing for sure.

Ty stepped out of the elevator, squeezed her shoulder, and faced her. "I know it's doubly official. Doc McAdams assured us twice that a summer solstice birth date is an accurate due date. We're going to be parents. Mom and Dad. Are you okay?"

Siobhan clutched her keys tighter. Would she be like her mother? Surly, argumentative and caustic during each of her pregnancies? She didn't want to be. Welcoming a child meant responsibilities, changes and joy. Parenting wasn't easy. Lupa, she knew that from raising her siblings. She wouldn't change that part of her life. This time would be different. It was her time. Time to embrace motherhood and experiencing the wonders of birth and nurturing her child. Wait, what had Doc McAdams said as he examined her?

"Ty, it's still sinking in. June birth. Summer Equinox and Solstice. Winter Solstice is tomorrow. Christmas two days later. So much change so fast. And Doc McAdams said multiples? What in the name of the One was he talking about?"

"Yeah, I damn near blurted out what the Lupa was he talking about?" Ty held out his hand. "Want me to drive?"

"No, thanks." Siobhan unlocked the car and got in. "Ty, I thought Doc McAdams was kidding about multiple births. Now I don't. Remember my sister Charlotte had twins and my cousin Syrene had triplets. Maybe we need to prepare for more than one?"

Ty closed the passenger door, fastened his seatbelt and glanced at her. "I remember something the midwife nurse told us in basic paramedic training. Always be prepared for more than what's known. Sure helped Keith when he ended up assisting two births in one night."

Siobhan put the car into gear. "Okay. We prepare for multiples. Doc's assistant made an ultrasound appointment for spring time. Guess we'll know more then."

"Now to break the news to Aunt Elana and James." Ty laughed. "Aunt Elana said it was time I started using her family designation since we were now sorta officially related."

"Don't think there's much news to break. Except more than one baby in the hatch. Wonder if Aunt Elana took birthing classes as part of her matchmaking training? Been a few rounded bellies matched up at the Sadie Hawkins events." Siobhan pulled out of the parking garage wondering how much more her life was going to change in the coming months.

Elana picked up her cell phone. Caller ID showed the moving truck's driver Gordon's number. "Hello, Gordon. Merry Solstice and Christmas to you."

"Thank you, Ms. Jones. Same to you and yours. Got some news and updates for you." Gordon's tone sounded jovial and upbeat.

"I hope it's good news." Elana motioned James to her as she put the phone on speaker. "My friend James is listening too. He's coordinating things with me."

"Greetings, sir. I've got updates and news for both of you then."

"Go ahead, Gordon." James sat on the couch next to Elana.

"Ms. Jones, we're a half-day out from Cauldron Falls. The team and I would like to unpack the truck tomorrow mid-morning. We've got family we'd like to spend Christmas with in town." Voices sounded in the background. Gordon's laughter boomed out of the speaker. "Zach says if we speed, we might make it sooner. I doubt any of us want to try explaining beating the speed limit to the cops."

James smiled, nodding as Gordon continued. "Ms. Jones, we'll meet you at your place around eleven-thirty tomorrow, okay?"

"All right by me. See you then. Drive carefully and be safe." Elana ended the call. She turned to James. "When is Amelia due back?"

"Not till after New Year's. She texted me a couple of days ago. Her text just got through due to the storm. Why?"

"That solidifies my idea. You can help me decide where the furniture goes. The movers will place it once, maybe twice. Then that's it." Elana smiled. "Hanging curtains and unpacking the basics is all on me. Could use a second set of eyes and hands. You willing? You always were the artsy one with a good eye for designing. You can also bunk with me until Amelia returns."

James laughed. "I went into electronics. Not interior design. I still dabble in things with a local designer from time to time. A little side job now and then supplements retirement income. Sure, I'll help. Maybe I won't want to bunk anywhere else when Amelia returns."

"I'll keep that under advisement." Elana hugged and kissed James. "I'll check on that closer to that time unless you tell me otherwise."

James kissed Elana twice. "You're on."

"Ty and Siobhan are due back soon. I've got their Solstice gifts to wrap. Do you need to do any last minute shopping or wrapping?"

"Lance's gift he gets on Christmas. His preference. Solstice for him was about smores and hot dogs cooked over the fireplace fire. Around midnight, Amelia often made peppermint hot chocolate and served her almond maple bundt cake. We'd make up stories with Lance's help. He wanted memories of good times and family, not his father walking out and not returning."

"Sorry to hear that. I don't get why people do that." Elana pulled on her coat. "What can I add to your gift for Lance? What do you think you want to add to mine for Siobhan and Ty?"

"Gift cards for Lance. He's never sure what he wants and like he says gift cards are nice for those spur-of-the-moment purchases especially when things are on sale. " James put on his coat and picked up his watch cap. "I think gift cards for Ty are probably a good idea. For Siobhan, I would like to get a couple of gift cards for her to be able to use for things like a crib and kid clothes. Better off with one of the department stores that also lets you shop online."

"Pierre dropped their car keys off with me in case we needed to run errands. I'm glad Siobhan decided to close Sadie's until Chef and Pierre could check things out. Driving their aunt's new car is an opportunity Chef and Pierre didn't want to miss."

"You bet new car smell and luxury is a treat when you can do it." James followed her out the door. As they approached the car, James asked, "Do you want me to drive? I've got the smaller edition of this at home."

"Not necessary. Car transport delivered my car to the storage facility before the storm." Elana faced James, grinning as she continued speaking. "Getting a small car made sense instead of my 5-speed sedan. Change of life included change of vehicles."

James chortled. "That's my Elana. Practical and thoughtful."

"Used to overthink things too much." Elana started the car. "Learned you can only plan so much. Gotta build in flexibility."

James let out a low wolfish whistle. "You are turning me on, lady. Practical, flexible and smart. Batting three for three. *You're a catch*!"

"Thank you. So are you, my dear." Elana pulled out of the parking lot and headed towards downtown Cauldron Falls.

TWENTY-FIVE

James tucked the small box into the pocket of his coat. Elana had admired several of the items in the jewelry store as they window shopped. Lunch with Siobhan and Ty had delayed shopping until they parted company after agreeing to meet at the parking structure in two hours. He caught sight of Ty stuffing a bag with the jewelry store's logo on it into his jacket pocket. Elana had the bags from their joint purchases. She had gone into a store stating she wanted to look at something she'd noticed on a rack. That had given him the time he needed to finish up his purchase. Solstice and Christmas presents shopping was done. He and Elana agreed that next year they were doing it early and better informed. James started walking toward the exit to the parking structure.

"Come on. Let's head home." Elana said, matching his pace. "Siobhan wasn't sure what to get Ty for Solstice and Christmas. We settled on a play toy chest."

James chuckled. "Yeah keeping their play toys other than the guest room is a great idea."

"I told her we found them." Elana laughed. "Siobhan still blushes nicely.

"You mean I missed it?" James stopped. "Elana, you are naughty."

"No, just truthful." Elana held her hand out to James. "She did turn a lovely shade of pink."

"I hope you didn't let on about our big gift." James clasped Elana's hand.

"No. Part of the gift is customizing it with the name." Elana sighed. "Siobhan said she and Ty had their holiday shopping done as well."

"Good. We got in and out without having to deal with the crowds too much." James stopped in front of the restaurant close to the exit. He inhaled and glanced at Elana. "Sure smells good."

"You really want to deal with the noise and all those people?" Ty asked walking up. Siobhan with him.

"I've got a better idea." Siobhan held her phone. "I got a text from Chef and Pierre asking if we wanted to join them, their aunt and her husband for a potluck dinner. We can bring dessert or a side dish to share. Chef is making his crock pot chicken legs with his homemade barbecue sauce plus his aunt's from scratch yeast rolls with cinnamon butter."

"The bakery is still open. I can get a cake." Elana started back toward the bakery near the restaurant.

Siobhan followed her aunt. "Yeah, a couple gallons of their apple pear cider would go well. Ty? James? What you bringing?"

James looked at Ty. Ty shrugged. "Looks like we got the vegetables sides to deal with."

"Hey, what about potato salad and cole slaw? The takeout place has quarts of both available." James headed toward the food court. "Come on, Ty. Even baked beans sound good."

"Great ideas," Ty said, following James. "I'll get some crab cakes from the Japanese place too."

Fifteen minutes later, James and Ty regrouped with Elana and Siobhan back at the exit. James packed the food bags in the back seat of the car. Ty and Siobhan had one more stop to make before they met them at home. James closed the door and inhaled.

"If we didn't make it to Chef and Pierre's, we got the makings of a wonderful dinner ourselves." His stomach loudly growled its agreement as he fastened his seatbelt.

"No sampling or snacking before or after we get home." Elana pulled out of the parking structure and turned onto the main street, heading out of downtown.

"Did Siobhan and Ty say where they were going?" James reached back and rattled one of the food bags.

"James, I said no snacking." Elana glanced at James as she pulled up to a stop sign. "You misbehaving?"

"Being a little naughty. Rattling bags got your attention." James leaned over and kissed her cheek. "Anyway, where are Siobhan and Ty going?"

"You getting protective?" Elana chortled. "They're going to pick up Chef and Pierre's anniversary gift for their aunt and her husband. A handmade wooden frame and picture collage from their wedding."

"Nice!" James patted his coat pocket. He hoped Elana said yes when she unwrapped her gift.

He turned on the radio, found a holiday music station and they sang along as they drove the rest of the way to the condo.

Elana's phone chimed as she and James pulled into the condo's parking lot. She handed James her phone. "Please see who that is while I park."

"Caller ID isn't well lit."James held up the phone, squinting at the caller ID. "I think Siobhan is calling."

"Put her on speaker." Elana pulled into the closest parking space to Chef and Pierre's aunt's building.

"Hi, Aunt Elana." Siobhan's voice boomed out of the speaker. "What is that echo?"

"Got you on speaker." Elana put the car into park and shut it off. "Something up?"

"Not really." Siobhan laughed. "Ty and I decided we need a Solstice Christmas tree. A bit of yule and a bit of the secular holiday. It'll fit on the side table. We can decorate it after dinner."

"How much longer you going to be?" James glanced at his watch. They were due to gather for dinner in thirty minutes.

"We're ten minutes out," Ty called out. "If James helps me get the tree and decorations inside, Siobhan can bring our bags in."

"All right. James and I will get our bags and the food bags in." Elana opened the driver's door. "We can use the inside hallway to get to Chef and Pierre's. See you soon."

James ended the call and handed Elana her phone. "I can grab most of the food bags from my side. What about you?"

"Maybe Siobhan and Ty can help out with placing stuff and getting things unpacked." James closed the driver's and passenger-side back doors.

Elana stomped the snow off her boots as she reached the sidewalk. James held the door for her. She pushed the elevator up button and faced James.

Elevator opened as Siobhan and Ty entered the lobby. Fifteen minutes later, all the packages and the food bags were in, they exited the elevator into the interior hallway leading to the next-door building where Chef and Pierre's Aunt Stella lived.

James rapped twice on the condo door, marked sixteen fifty-two. Chef opened the door. His usual immaculate appearance gone. His hair stood up in places. Yelling and cussing sounded in the background. Chef glanced over his shoulder and back at them with a weak smile. "Come on in. Welcome. Glad you could make it."

Elana nudged James and whispered, "Offer to come back later."

"No need for that," Chef quickly replied. "Wolf hearing, Elana. Aunt Stella is trying to outdo Pierre on a family recipe. She made me a chef's hat for my Solstice gift. Just took it off."

Siobhan stepped around James and Elana. "Chef, is this the shortbread cookie recipe? Or the Angel food pound cake one?"

"Both. Aunt Stella took her hearing aid off. Pierre is reading the recipe to her. His batch of shortbread is in the oven. Aunt Stella keeps telling him he's reading the Angel food pound cake recipe wrong. "

"Two pound pound cake?" Ty asked, moving closer to Siobhan.

"No, double batch. Meaning more cake. Like four loaf pans worth." Chef stepped back from the door. "Look at it this way: fresh baked goods for your Solstice morning breakfast as Pierre's, mine, and Aunt Stella's gift to you."

"We'll stay out of the way." Siobhan handed Chef her coat. "What is Ethan doing?"

"Making the maple syrup frosting for the pound cakes." Chef motioned Siobhan closer. "Said he wasn't going near that kitchen until either the smoke alarm took off or Aunt Stella sat down at the table."

Siobhan chortled. "He's making the frosting for the pound cakes and taking his time. Smart move."

Chef laid everyone's coats and jackets on the chair near the door.

"We brought baked beans, potato salad, mac and cheese, some cider, and a bakery cake." James held up the food bags.

"Plus crab and rice cakes from the Japanese restaurant." Ty held up his bag.

Chef rubbed his hands together. "Two crock pots full of chicken thighs and my homemade bourbon barbecue sauce. Two baking sheets of yeast rolls. Cinnamon butter warmed, ready to spread on them. Your add-ons give us enough food for seconds and thirds each."

Ethan entered the living room. "Welcome everyone. Come out to the dining room. I've got the cider pot warming. I heard someone mention cider."

James held his hand out to Ethan. "I'm James. Elana's full moon match. The cider is from Morgan's. Siobhan said their apple pear blended cider warmed and poured over mulling spices with a cinnamon stick was worth buying three gallons."

Ethan shook James's hand. "She's right. You have to know how to mix the mulling spices and when to add the cinnamon sticks as you pour the cider into the warming pot. Come with me, James. I'll share my family's mulled cinnamon spiced cider recipe with you."

"I'll go help them." Ty kissed Siobhan's cheek and followed James and Ethan into the dining room.

Chef turned to Elana and Siobhan. "Do you mind setting the table while I check on Pierre and Aunt Stella? It's gotten too quiet in there."

Elana shook her head. "Don't smell smoke. Too quiet might be a good thing. Yes, Siobhan and I will take care of setting the table."

Twenty minutes later, everyone sat down. Center of the table in a row were platters of chicken legs, bowls of potato salad, cole slaw and baked beans, a tray of yeast rolls and cinnamon butter, and a double-handled pot of mulled spiced cinnamon cider.

Chef tapped on his glass. He stood and raised his glass. "Here's too good food. Home cooking and sides from our fave restaurants. Awesome friends and family. Blessed Solstice eve all. Enjoy!"

"Chicken please." James handed Elana his plate. "Who won the baking cook-off?"

Elana forked two chicken legs onto James's plate. "Four pound cakes, maple frosting made and a hearing aid found on the back of the sink."

James pressed his lips tighter together as Ty added. "Six quarts of cider mulled and spiced, crab and rice cakes nicely diced and no bloodshed."

"Pierre, what are they singing about?" Aunt Stella asked from the head of the table.

"Praising the food and company." Pierre winked at Chef and tapped his thigh.

"Right, Aunt Stella." Chef pinched Pierre's leg as he continued, "Everyone is deciding who to team up with for the shortbread and holiday cookie decorating contest."

Siobhan looked at Ethan. He shrugged and grinned. "Let's hope Stella doesn't decide we're playing poker. She's been practicing all week with me. I've lost my allowance to quote her for the next fifteen full moons."

Three hours passed as they ate, discussed Cauldron Falls' position with the matchmakers' council, possible upcoming election candidates and got Aunt Stella to take a rain check on her poker winnings.

Siobhan tossed her jacket on the couch. "Put the cake and cookies in the fridge with the leftovers. I'm calling it a night."

"I'll take care of that." Elana took the two bags off the couch. "The load of laundry I did for all of us is in the dryer. I'll bring it out."

"I think we're all ready to sleep." Ty yawned and stretched. "We can put up the tree tomorrow."

"Sounds good to me." James stood as Elana came back with the basket full of clothes. "I'll help you fold."

Elana dumped the basket on the couch. Siobhan and Ty sorted out their clothes and folded them. James helped Elana fold theirs. Siobhan handed Ty his clothes and picked up hers. "Thanks, Aunt Elana, for helping out. We'll see you in the morning. Solstice gift exchange after breakfast?"

"Yes." Elana put her and James's clothes in the basket. "I almost forgot. James and I need to be at my townhouse midday tomorrow. The movers are unloading."

Siobhan hugged her. "Awesome. Ty and I will help you. Pierre and Chef are checking on Sadie's. Said they didn't need my help. Good night."

"Happy to help out." Ty hugged her. "Good night, Aunt Elana and James."

Elana set the basket on the dresser. "Tomorrow, James we begin a new phase of our lives."

"Sure are sweetie. A new adventure together." James shucked his clothes and got into bed.

Elana did the same. Soon, sleep enveloped them.

TWENTY-SIX

James refilled his mug with coffee. The remnants of two pieces of pound cake and shortbread plus scrambled eggs and toast sat on his plate. Decorating the Solstice tree generated laughs and opinions and a few fake spats. The silver star atop the tree finished the project. He smirked.

Putting up a tree had been a family tradition until his father and mother argued over whether it should be a yule tree or a Christmas one. He and Amelia didn't care. They dubbed it the holiday tree. Decorating it with mundane items that represented mortal and magic traditions balanced out the symbols each of them held near and dear. Amelia's late husband followed the secular calendar and partial religious observations. Amelia told their parents more than once that belief was more unified than they thought. James sat down next to Elana and started eating.

Elana put her fork down, wiped her mouth and drank the rest of her coffee. "What a fun way to start out Solstice."

"Ty wanted a bigger tree. I think this one is great." Siobhan warmed her coffee. She held up her piece of pound cake. "Aunt Stella's recipe is worth getting. Add this to Sadie's brunch menu, and it will be sold out."

"Check with Pierre and Chef." Ty stood up. "I'll start the dishes. We need to leave in thirty minutes."

James rose, picked up his and Elana's plates. "I'll help with the washing and drying."

Elana handed James Siobhan's plate and mug. "Siobhan, have you thought about hiring an assistant bartender? An assistant manager?"

Siobhan stretched. "Not really. Doc McAdams gave me a mid-June delivery time frame. He estimates I'm about three to four months along. Time to think about hiring after first of the year, I guess."

"Keep in mind you can go a month in either direction with the first one. You were two weeks over nine months." Elana stood. "Time to trade my pajamas for going-out clothes."

"Yeah, me too." Siobhan hugged her and entered her bedroom.

Elana pushed her bedroom door closed. She quickly dressed and brushed her teeth. As she combed her hair, she noted it was more gray. She could color it, cut it and do plenty of things to disguise her age. Why would she? James mentioned neither of them could turn back the hands of time this morning as they cuddled. Truth was, she didn't want to change her past. Parts of it hadn't been pleasant. She'd learned from the hard times. Embraced the change the lessons taught her and cherished the good times while celebrating the high points of those years with good friends and family. Coming home for the holidays was one of those high points. Seeing James again and taking a chance was proving one thing. Trusting her heart to someone else meant being vulnerable and open to hearing what that person had to say. Not putting her words into their thoughts or actions, aka making her translation theirs. Elana exited the bedroom, ready to step into a new phase of her life. A phase that included family and James.

Siobhan and Ty stood near the front door with their coats on. Elana looked around the living room. She picked up her coat off the back of a chair. "Where is James?"

"Bathroom," Ty blurted out. Siobhan rolled her eyes.

"I had to brush my teeth." James pulled on his watch cap. "I can't help it nature called at the same time."

Siobhan glanced at Elana. She shrugged and finished buttoning her coat. "Better here and now. Not halfway to the townhouse. Like you used to do as a kid."

"Oh, Lupa," Ty groaned. "I hope our children potty train early."

Elana busted out laughing. "Ty, get through diaper duty first. Worry about potty training when they're two to three years old."

Siobhan patted Ty's cheek. "Dear, maybe we need to ask your family about your childhood hard-headedness. Your sister whispered you and a mule could have a contest to see who would out stubborn the other. She was betting on the mule losing."

"Why aren't *you* blushing?" Ty stepped back from Siobhan. "*You* started this conversation."

"I own my past." Siobhan clasped Ty's hand. "I'm not the one that blurted out bathroom like it was headline news."

James thrust his arm between Ty and Siobhan. "I started the potty humor. I apologize. We got a townhouse to organize. Let's get going, shall we?"

James opened the door and held his hand out to Elana. "Let's go see our new nude wrestling zone."

Ty turned to Siobhan. "I guess friskiness runs in your family. May we be that crazy and wild for each other when we reach their age."

"I agree." Siobhan fastened her fanny pack around her waist. "I'm curious to see their new nude wrestling zone too. Might give me some ideas for enhancing ours."

Ty followed Siobhan out the door, muttering under his breath, "I will not blush. I will not blush."

"Which townhouse is yours?' Siobhan asked, turning into the new townhouse development on the east side of Cauldron Falls.

"End unit with the moving truck and the muscular hunks milling around." Elana snuck a glance at James. She caught Ty's expression in the review mirror reflection. He kept looking at Siobhan. James reached over, squeezed her hand, and said, "Enjoy the eye candy, love. Getting hot and bothered might give us a reason to do a quickie trial session of the nude wrestling zone."

Siobhan snorted. "Enough TMI! You'll have Ty permanently blushing."

"You're a bit red yourself, Siobhan," Ty countered back.

"Nah, warming up watching the eye candy." Siobhan parked two places over from the truck. "Is this someone's assigned parking space?"

"I don't know. I hadn't read that part of the townhouse association's by-laws yet." Elana unfastened her seatbelt. "I'll find out soon enough. The transport company delivers my car tomorrow."

A tall male with red hair and wearing glasses approached the car. Elana got out. " Hello, Gordon."

"Hello, Ms. Jones. Glad we finally got here. Ed and Wes plus their cousins will unload the truck shortly. We thank you for being understanding. I apologize again for the breakdown." Gordon faced James who walked up beside Elana.

"Gordon, pleasure to meet you. I'm Elana's friend, James." James shook Gordon's hand.

"Likewise, sir. Glad there's an extra set of eyes." Gordon chuckled. "Makes reading box labels easier and putting them in the right rooms."

Ty pointed to a car pulling in next to Siobhan's car. "Looks like the realtor's here."

Gladys Armstrong exited her car, carrying a small portfolio and a medium-sized bag. "Elana Jones, I'm glad I get to deliver these to you. Your keys, the townhouse association by-laws and the first month's utility bills. Your rebate on the closing costs took care of the necessary deposits. I got the old set of keys from your neighbor back and had a locksmith change out the locks on all doors."

"Thank you, Gladys. I'm ready for the walk-through." Elana covered the short distance to the walkway leading to the townhouse. She glanced over her shoulder and found James keeping up with her. Gladys and Gordon followed a few paces behind James.

Siobhan elbowed Ty. "Come on. Let's check out this nude wrestling pit. We might want to borrow it some night."

Ty coughed, glanced around and trotted after Siobhan. If this was an indicator of what this part of Siobhan's family was like, Lupa help him if the rest were even a bit like Elana and Siobhan.

Elana put the key in the lock, grasped James's hand, and turned the key. A click sounded. She turned the knob and opened the door to her new home.

James moved up beside her. "Congratulations, sweetie. May you find moments of happiness, years filled with joy and contentment here. Welcome home."

Elana blinked, reached up and wiped a couple of tears away. Whatever the future held, she had a home. A place to call her own. A place that she owned. No more rental agreements. No more yearly rent increases. Best of all, it was hers. Paid for in full. "Thank you, James. Come with me and check out my home."

First floor contained the combination living room family room, eat-in kitchen, half-bath, and a den. A possible office library combination. A place where she could conduct her matchmaking business and put out her beloved books. A space to relax in and do business without having to reserve space, get someone's permission, and deal with nosy landlords or rental agents.

As she climbed the stairs leading to the second floor, James's hand touched hers. She hoped his hand touching hers continued nightly as they climbed the stairs together. They had much to discuss. Time for that would come once the movers had unpacked the truck and placed her furniture. After she and James, with Siobhan and Ty's help, hung curtains and put the starting touches of turning the townhouse into her home sweet home.

At the top of the steps, the door on the right led to the spacious master bedroom suite. Walk-in closets lined the short hallway leading to the master bathroom. The bathroom contained a glass-enclosed shower with a bench and two small shelves along the back wall for shampoo, soap and her mesh sponge, toilet, and pedal stool sink. The two large windows facing the east would allow ample sunlight to fill and warm the room. Two other medium-sized bedrooms with a shared bathroom completed the three-bedroom makeup of the upper floor.

Gladys, Gordon, Siobhan and Ty met her and James at the base of the stairs. Elana nodded as she spoke. "I approve. Let unpacking the truck begin."

Four hours later, Gordon, Wes and Ed waved goodbye as they pulled out. The living room, kitchen, and master bedroom were ready for living. The guest rooms needed linens and pillows. The shared second bathroom towels and accessories lined the counter, ready to put away in the next few days. Boxes of books stacked two and three deep lined the walls of the den. The built-in shelves would soon have new occupants. Her desk and chair were ready for her computer and monitor. Pots, pans and dishes cluttered the kitchen counter space waiting to settle into their cabinet space. Tomorrow was another day. A new beginning to her life. Her life in Cauldron Falls. It felt good to be home.

Elana faced Siobhan, Ty and James. "It's Solstice. Time to celebrate. Let's head back. Tomorrow is soon enough to do more here."

Forty minutes later, they pulled into the condo's parking lot. Another twenty found them seated at the table, breaking chunks of bread off two french bread loaves, dipping them into a rich homemade chicken stew and toasting each other with leftover mulled spiced cider.

James rinsed out the sink and hung the dish towel on the oven door. "Doing dishes by hand and sharing the chore is more fun than loading the dishwasher."

Elana chortled. "I remember my Mom kept asking me if Dad was planning on cooking his own meal and mentioned the dishwasher more than once. He could "

"Cleaning up the kitchen behind your Dad was something else." James kissed Elana's cheek. "Let's go unwrap presents. I unwrapped and wrapped one of mine this morning. If you know what I mean."

"Oh, I do." Elana winked. "Did help with the unwrapping and rewrapping of one of mine too."

"Aunt Elana. James," Siobhan called out from the living room. "Time to open Solstice gifts."

TWENTY-SEVEN

Siobhan laid another present at the base of the tree on the right-hand side. She stepped back, nodding and smiling. "Okay, presents divvied up."

Ty sat on the couch. "Why divvied up?"

"Family tradition." Siobhan sat beside Ty. "As my brothers and sisters got married and had families of their own, Solstice and Christmas became intermingled. Human traditions, magical celebrations and supernatural observations rolled into one."

"Several of Siobhan's and my relatives mingled celebrations together in respectful ways like divvying up the gifts. Some opened on Solstice and some on Christmas." Elana sat in the chair next to the couch. "Showing respect for traditions and beliefs kept the peace and taught us about diversity. Everyone has value."

"Going gray early got me in on Christmas celebrations through a good minister friend of mine from college." James sat in the chair opposite the couch. "Dressed up like Santa Claus and helped pass out presents and care packages to the needy. Seeing the joy and happiness that brought others gave me joy and happiness as well.

Siobhan stood, pointing to the presents. "Left is Solstice. Right is Christmas."

She picked up the small envelope. "This is for us, Ty."

Siobhan laid the envelope on the coffee table. "Ty, you pick out a gift and say who's it for. We open the gifts after they're distributed."

Ty got up, rubbing his hands together. "Okay, I am going for this large one back here."

He pulled out a large present wrapped in two different kinds of paper. One side was bright yellow, red and green lights adorning holiday wreaths. The other side was silver and gold stars on a blue background. "The tag reads for Aunt Elana and James."

Elana took the box and leaned it against the chair. "My turn since my name was first on the tag."

She picked up a medium-sized envelope. "This is for Siobhan."

Siobhan laid the envelope with the other. "Let James go next since his name was on the joint package."

James stood. "Hmmm. Lots of envelopes. A few more wrapped gifts."

He picked up an envelope and the small box next to it. "The sticker on the envelope matches the paper. They're both for Siobhan and Ty."

Turns continued until each had an almost equal number of gifts or envelopes.

"Siobhan, James and I have a special gift for you and Ty that couldn't be wrapped." Elana stood and reached behind her chair. She pulled out a small multi-colored basket. "You're going to receive a lot of small gifts and/or gift cards. This is a special place for you to keep them. It's divided in the middle. One side for your gift cards and the other for the baby."

Siobhan knuckled a tear off her cheek. "Aunt Elana—James—Thank you both. This basket looks familiar."

Elana hugged Siobhan as she handed her the basket. "It should. It's the same one your great-grandma kept your hairbands and diaper pins in when she babysat you. A gift from those that went on before you and a gift to those that are yet to come."

"I think you'll want to open up the first envelope and the last one next." James scooted to the edge of his seat.

Siobhan tore open the small envelope first. "Ty, it's from Pierre and Chef. A hundred dollar gift card to the baby furniture shop in Sylvan Valley. The one that specializes in local artisans' products."

"Awesome," Ty said, pointing to the basket. "First entry for our baby."

Siobhan nodded, placing the card in one side of the basket. She quickly opened the second larger envelope. "Aunt Elana and James, thank you! A year's worth of baby photos plus a crib with the baby's name engraved on it also from the Sylvan Valley shop."

Ty picked up one of his presents and tore off the wrapping paper. He laughed. "Siobhan, you are too much. A year's worth of dry cleaning for my uniforms and a new set of gym workout clothes. Thank you!"

Gift opening continued until a trash bag of wrapping paper sat close to the tree. Several gift cards filled each side of Siobhan's basket. Blankets and newborn clothes lay on the arm of the couch. Elana held up the two curios Siobhan and Ty got her. Two black cats. One wore a witch's hat with a full moon on top of it. The other wore a glitter collar. James's gifts consisted of gift cards to local stores and a bathrobe from Elana.

Elana yawned as she picked up a similar colored bathrobe to James's robe. "James, thank you for the robe. Ty and Siobhan for the new bath and kitchen towels. Gift cards will be used to decorate my new place. I am heading to bed."

Siobhan and Ty hugged her and James good night.

James shut the bedroom door behind him. Elana sat on the bed, watching him. He sat down next to her, entwining his fingers with hers as he spoke. "I'm sorry," he began. Elana leaned over and kissed him. Silencing what else he might have said.

Elana cupped his cheek. "There's nothing to be sorry about. We acted on our free will. Enjoyed some awesome cuddles and loving. Ended the evening with a match declaration. I don't see anything to be sorry about."

James blinked. Apologizing had been in his thoughts since he stepped up and made the public declaration before the matchmaking portion of the evening started. Getting back together with Elana was something he thought about often. Here they were together again. He had yet to declare his heart's intent. The reason he stepped up, followed through with the public declaration and full moon recording. The unsaid murmurings his psyche and heartfelt yearnings cried out each time he touched and held Elana. Making love with her was awesome. The connection and sparks were different. They were different. He'd read her aura twice as she, Tara, Naomi and Zelda invoked Luna and the One's blessings on the proceedings and crystals they used for their matchmaking.

"Elana," James said, facing her. "There's a part of me that needs to apologize. Not for today or declaring our match before discussing it with you."

"Okay. Go on. I'm listening."

James cupped Elana's hands between his. "I walked away when we were having problems. You were going one way and me another. I was caught up in what was right for me instead of what was right for us."

"James, both of us were selfish. I needed my independence. You needed someone who would back you. We talked, but we didn't listen. I owe you an apology, too. Can you forgive me?"

James leaned in, brushed his lips across Elana's and pulled back. "Darling, I forgive you and me. I forgive us. I've got more to tell you."

Elana pressed her fingers against his lips. "Before you do, I want you to know I forgive us too and me for being self-centered and cutting you off."

James kissed Elana's fingers and nodded. Elana lowered her hand. "Go on with what you need to tell me."

"I almost didn't come home for the holidays. I was ready to tell Amelia no when she invited me. I'm glad I changed my mind." James looped his arms around Elana's neck. "Coming home for the holidays, I got the best present next to being with family, you and being able to tell you an amazing surprise."

"A surprise?" Elana leaned back. Her gaze met his dead on.

"Yes, Elana Jones, I love you. Have for a long time. Stubbornness kept me from telling you. Now you know. I'm giving you a large part of my heart. I hope you'll cherish and take care of it."

Elana reached up and wiped a tear off her cheek. James lowered one arm. She quickly laid her hand on the one still around her neck. "These are tears of happiness. I'd given up finding you again only because I was focused on my work. What I thought made me happy. Other men piqued my interest from time to time. None of them were you. When I admitted that I was comparing them to you, I quit looking."

"Why didn't you look for me? Reach out to Amelia on how to get a hold of me?"

"Pride. Scared you'd gotten married. Found someone else." James got down on one knee and fished the item he had carried in his pocket all day out. He slowly opened the box and clasped Elana's hand. "I have one more present for you. Will you marry me?"

Elana glanced from him to the box and back to him. "Are you sure?"

James took the ring out of the box and put it on Elana's right ring finger. He stood and started shucking his clothes. "Previously, I would have said woman let's get naked and cuddle. Now I'm asking as I bare it all, Elana, will you be nude with me, cuddle, sleep beside me and if we both want to make love, not just sex. Join our bodies together for mutual pleasure. I am very, very sure. "

Grinning, Elana rose, stripping off clothing as she answered. "Yes, I'll marry you. See I love you too. Being nude with you, even naked, is delicious and necessary for me. Nude snuggling is the best kind. Making love with mutual desire between us is a heady turn-on. I'm ready, willing, and the answer is yes when you are."

Not caring where their clothes landed, each helped the other finish undressing. Cover tossed back, Elana got in and scooted to the middle of the bed, making room for James. He laid down beside her, not quite touching her.

"I'm glad we came home for the holidays." James pulled the covers over them.

"So am I." Elana closed the space between them, cuddling closer to James.

EPILOGUE

Sadie's—Christmas Morning

"New tradition starting," Siobhan grinned as Pierre and Chef loaded the buffet with brunch items. "Christmas Day Brunch. Recipes from Pierre and Chef's families. Aunt Stella's recipes."

The kitchen door creaked as it swung open. Aunt Stella, followed by Ethan, both wearing chef's hats with their names embroidered on them, came out pushing the two-tiered cart. On top were several trays of baked goods: Shortbread cookies, cheese danish and yeast rolls stuffed with sausage and cheese. The second shelf held sheet pans of sliced pound cake topped with maple frosting.

Ty stood next to Siobhan, grinning and patting his shirt pocket from time to time. The print shirt he wore was a gift from Lance and his mom. His mom had sewn shirts for each of them from yard goods she'd found at a closeout sale. Each shirt's print was cars and items from their teens. A stroll down memory lane for each whenever they wore them is what the card enclosed with the shirt read.

He glanced to where Elana and James stood, ready to hand out utensils and plates to the two lines of the fifty matches from the Sadie Hawkins full moon event, waiting to enter the buffet area. James and Elana announced their engagement on the drive over. The one-carat solitaire diamond Elana wore sparkled each time one of the overhead lights illuminated it. A similar cut diamond studded stick pin decorated James's shirt pocket.

Siobhan moved to the head of the lines, standing between her aunt and James. "Today, we begin a new tradition. A new start for Sadie's. A new phase of business. Christmas Day Brunch for the December Sadie Hawkins full moon matches." She picked up a pair of scissors, held them aloft and spoke. "On the count of three, I cut the serving line ribbon."

"One," the crowd called out.

Siobhan lowered the scissors some.

"Two," the crowd chanted louder.

Siobhan lowered the scissors very close to the ribbon.

"Hold," a male voice from the back of the line called out. Everyone turned as Caleb and Maggie made their way through the line. Murmurs sounded. Were Maggie and Caleb holding hands? Walking side by side? Maggie was smiling? Caleb as well?

Caleb turned as he reached Ty. "Cousin, you ready?"

Ty glanced at Siobhan and back to Caleb. "Yes. You?"

Caleb held up his hand, palm toward Ty. Caleb winked. "I sure am."

Ty ducked under the ribbon Elana, and James held aloft.

"Siobhan, we've been through a lot together. Friends, lovers and soon-to-be parents." Ty turned, kneeled, and pulled the box out of his shirt pocket. "Two full moon matches, and I know you're the one. The one I want to spend the rest of my life with, raise our children with and grow old with. I love you. Will you marry me?"

Siobhan blinked twice. She held out her hand as she spoke, "Ty, yes, I will raise our children with you. Spend my life with you and grow old with you. I love you, too."

Chattering and more murmurs sounded.

Caleb held up his hand. "Maggie, life is full of chances and challenges. Risks and rewards. You're a reward worth treasuring. Partnering with and seeing what comes next. They say love comes with time. Others say listen to your heart. I hear mine saying love has found the one. I hope you feel the same. Will you spend the rest of your life with me as my wife and partner?"

"I come to this as your partner. Your equal in many things. We will work out what needs figuring out. We stand together stronger than either of us did separately." Maggie turned around, looked at the crowd and faced Caleb. She placed one hand over her heart and lowered it to her waist. "I hope our child isn't as stubborn and opinionated as we are."

Cheers sounded as Siobhan cut the ribbon. Ty slipped her engagement ring on her finger as couples started milling past them. Caleb and Maggie exchanged their engagement rings.

Elana slipped her arm around James and hugged him tightly. Luna and the One had brought many together for the holidays. Coming home for the holidays was one of the best decisions she and James made.

Don't miss out!

Visit the website below and you can sign up to receive emails whenever Solara Gordon publishes a new book. There's no charge and no obligation.

https://books2read.com/r/B-A-RAUJ-ZIDSC

BOOKS 2 READ

Connecting independent readers to independent writers.

Did you love *Home for the Holidays*? Then you should read *A Christmas Reunion*[1] by Solara Gordon!

Welcome to Cauldron Falls, where full moon matches and Sadie Hawkins dances ignite sparks and join hearts as the magic of love fills the air. Toss in a matchmaking aunt's dinner invitation postscript, "come with a date or get paired up with any solo attendee", and finding a date becomes a priority.

Ryan Butler is all set with planning and cooking the family Christmas dinner. Finding a dinner date is an issue until he runs into his ex, Kate Ferndale. Kate's plans to help with the Christmas Sadie Hawkins dance don't include getting matched or attending the family dinner with her ex, Ryan.

With full moon sparks and love magic in the air a week before Christmas, is a Christmas Reunion for Kate and Ryan in the air?

Read more at https://solaragordon.com/.

Also by Solara Gordon

Cascade Bay
Love Reborn
Reunited By Choice
Love's Triple Play
Three Hearts In Love
For the Love of Three

Cauldron Falls
Believe In Love
Home for the Holidays
A Christmas Reunion

Peyton Corners
Falling for You
Caught by Love's Slow Burn

Standalone
A Heart's Desire
To Love You Again
To Love You Again

Watch for more at https://solaragordon.com/.

About the Author

Solara loves and lives with her partner of 21 years in the Metro DC area. What started out as a bi-coastal romance soon settled on one coast.

A vivid imagination keeps her busy creating her next fascinating romance. She enjoys creating unique characters and watching their journeys unfold. "Love freely given multiplies and will return endlessly" is a key aspect of her stories. Add in alternative lifestyles and her love for the paranormal, and the uncommon becomes the norm in many of her stories.

Her day job in the financial services industry pays the bills while she pens her erotic tales.

Read more at https://solaragordon.com/.